THE ISLAND OF DR. LIBRIS

OTHER BOOKS BY CHRIS GRABENSTEIN

Escape from Mr. Lemoncello's Library
A *New York Times* bestseller

THE HAUNTED MYSTERY SERIES
The Crossroads
Winner of the Agatha Award and the Anthony Award

The Hanging Hill
Winner of the Agatha Award

The Smoky Corridor

The Black Heart Crypt
Winner of the Agatha Award

the ISLAND of DR. LIBRIS

CHRIS GRABENSTEIN

RANDOM HOUSE NEW YORK

This is a work of fiction. Names, characters, places, and incidents either are the product of the author's imagination or are used fictitiously. Any resemblance to actual persons, living or dead, events, or locales is entirely coincidental.

 Published in the United States by
Random House Children's Books, a division of Random House LLC,
a Penguin Random House Company, New York.

Random House and the colophon are registered trademarks of
Random House LLC.

Visit us on the Web! randomhousekids.com

Educators and librarians, for a variety of teaching tools, visit us at
RHTeachersLibrarians.com

Library of Congress Cataloging-in-Publication Data
Grabenstein, Chris.
The island of Dr. Libris / Chris Grabenstein. —First edition.
pages cm.
Summary: A twelve-year-old boy, worried that his parents may divorce, discovers that an island in the middle of the lake where he is spending the summer is the testing grounds of the mysterious Dr. Libris, who may have invented a way to make the characters in books come alive.
ISBN 978-0-385-38844-3 (trade) — ISBN 978-0-385-38846-7 (lib. bdg.) —
ISBN 978-0-385-38847-4 (ebook) — ISBN 978-0-553-53843-4 (intl. tr. pbk.)
[1. Inventions—Fiction. 2. Characters in literature—Fiction.
3. Books and reading—Fiction. 4. Divorce—Fiction.] I. Title.
II. Title: The island of Doctor Libris.
PZ7.G7487Is 2015 [Fic]—dc23 2014000214

Printed in the United States of America
10 9 8 7 6 5 4 3 2 1
First Edition

Random House Children's Books supports
the First Amendment and celebrates the right to read.

For Uncle Julian and Aunt Patsy,
who lived such storied lives.
And for you, the reader.
Thank you for volunteering to
attempt this feat of magic with me.

THE ISLAND OF DR. LIBRIS

THE THETA PROJECT

Lab Note #316

Prepared by

Dr. Xiang Libris, PsyD, DLit

I am thrilled to report that after an exhaustive search, I have found the ideal subject for our first field test, which will commence as soon as Billy G., a twelve-year-old male with a very vivid imagination, arrives on-site.

His mother will be busy. His father will be away. He will be bored.

In short, Billy G. will be perfect.

Billy Gillfoyle's dad shifted gears and gunned the engine.

"Hang on, kiddo!" he shouted over the roar. "Sign says 'Curves Ahead.' "

The convertible rocketed up the winding country road like it was the Space Lizard's Galaxy Blaster from Billy's favorite comic books.

"Woo-hoo!" cried Billy.

The top was down. Wind whipped through Billy's hair. Gravel spewed out from under the tires. Bugs splattered on the windshield.

It was awesome.

His dad was awesome. No, his dad was *fun*!

His mother?

Well, she had to be more serious, because she was a math professor, not a writer of cool TV commercials like his dad. But together they were kind of perfect.

At least Billy thought so. His parents? Not so much.

That was why Billy would be spending the summer with his mom but not his dad.

In a cabin.

On a lake.

In the middle of nowhere.

His mom was already there. His dad would haul Billy up to the cabin, then whip back around to spend the summer at their apartment in New York City.

Billy wished they could all be together, but there was nothing he could do to change his parents' minds. After all, he was just a kid.

He sank a little lower in his seat as his dad piloted the screaming convertible through the road's breakneck curves. Yup. Even the car had more power than Billy.

"Have you been getting enough sleep, hon?" his mother asked while Billy's dad emptied the car.

Billy stood in what he figured was the lake cottage's front yard—a scraggly patch of weeds and dirt.

People always thought Billy needed a nap, because he had heavy-lidded eyes and a long, droopy face.

"I'm fine, Mom."

"Okay," his mother said with a smile that looked like it hurt. "Well, welcome to Lake Katrine. I think you'll like it up here. We have a dock out back and a rowboat."

Billy nodded. He wasn't all that big on water sports.

"You can go exploring out on the island," she added.

"Great." Billy played along. He didn't want to make his mom feel sadder than he could tell she already did.

"Oh, I nearly forgot. I saw some other kids in the cottages on either side of ours. Two of the boys look like they're your age. Maybe you guys will become friends this summer."

Billy's dad hauled over Billy's suitcase. "That should do it."

"Thank you, Bill," his mother said politely.

"No problem, Kim." His dad stared off at the sparkling water behind the cabin. "Good old Lake Katrine."

"I'm surprised you remember it."

"Definitely. But I don't remember this cabin. Who'd you rent it from? Davy Crockett?"

He had a point. Billy's home for the next ten weeks looked like it had been built out of jumbo-sized Lincoln Logs. The screened-in porch was filled with furniture made from bent tree branches. Also—and this was sort of weird—security cameras were mounted all over the place: under the eaves of the gable roof, up in the nook of a nearby tree, over in the far corner of the porch.

Their little red lights blinked at Billy.

"I rented it from Dr. Libris," said Billy's mother.

"Who's he?" asked Billy.

"Dr. Xiang Libris. He also owns the island out in the middle of the lake."

"*Shihahng?*" said Billy.

"It's Chinese and spelled with an 'X.' Dr. Libris is a professor at my college. Since he won't be coming up here this summer, I was able to rent his cabin at a very reasonable price."

She narrowed her eyes a little when she said that last bit.

Because Billy's dad wasn't very good at managing money. Billy had learned this (and wished he hadn't) by listening to his parents argue late at night when they thought he was asleep.

Apparently, his dad spent too much money on "silly toys."

And, according to Billy's dad, his mom needed to "lighten up," "relax," and not "crunch so many numbers."

Maybe I could win the lottery, thought Billy. *Then all their money problems would disappear.*

In his mind, Billy could see it: Him holding a jumbo-sized cardboard check for fifty million dollars. His parents hugging and kissing each other and agreeing with the governor that it was okay, just this once, for a twelve-year-old kid to be the Mega Lotto Jackpot winner.

"Well," said Billy's dad, "I'd better go. We have a client meeting first thing tomorrow." He hopped into the convertible. "See you in a couple weeks, kiddo!"

And with one last wave, Billy's father sped down the road, his tires spitting gravel the whole way.

"Did you stop for lunch?" Billy's mom asked as he lugged his suitcase up the steps to the porch.

"Yeah."

"No wonder you guys were late. Did your father take you to the Red Barn?"

"No. Burger Maxx."

His mom wrinkled her nose.

"Hey," said Billy, "if he writes the commercials, he has to eat the food. It's the law."

She smiled.

"So, what's the Red Barn?" Billy asked.

"A cozy spot over on Route Seventeen. They bake the best blueberry pie on the planet. Your dad and I used to go there when we were dating. We'd rent a car, drive up to Lake Katrine, and eat pie."

Now his mom had a faraway look in her eye. Billy

wondered if she ever shut out the real world and imagined a better one like he did.

But just as quickly as she slipped away, she zipped back.

"If you get hungry before dinner, you can fix yourself a snack." She led Billy into the kitchen and opened a cupboard.

Two whole shelves were lined with bright orange-and-red cartons of shrink-wrapped peanut butter crackers—just about the only food Billy, who was kind of skinny, actually enjoyed eating.

"Promise me you'll also eat at least two pieces of fruit every day?"

"Deal," said Billy.

"Here. Tuck a couple into your backpack. I don't want you starving when you're out having fun."

"Thanks."

"So why don't you settle in and poke around? I need to go back upstairs and work on my dissertation."

A dissertation, Billy had learned, was a very long, very boring paper that nobody would ever read except the professors who would decide whether his mom was "smart enough to be called *Dr.* Gillfoyle" and earn more money.

The paper was so complicated Billy's mother planned to work on it *all summer*. That meant Billy would need to find lots of things to do on his own.

"Don't worry about me," he said. "I'll be fine."

"I know, Billy. You always are."

* * *

Billy hauled his suitcase up to the second floor.

After bumping the rolling bag up each and every one of the very steep steps, he reached his bedroom. The walls were paneled with knotty pine. There was a flannel blanket on the bed. The rug featured fish. Billy felt like he'd just walked into some kind of outdoor-clothing catalog.

Except there was another security camera suspended from the ceiling. Billy wondered if Dr. Libris was worried about people stealing his duck decoy lamps.

He rummaged around in his suitcase and found his bathing suit.

He didn't fold it up and put it in the chest of drawers.

He hung it over the lens of that creepy spy camera and headed back downstairs to check out the living room.

It was pretty much a bust.

No TV, DVD player, or Xbox. No computer whatsoever.

There was, however, a framed needlework sampler hanging on the wall over the sofa:

A book is proof that humans
are capable of working magic.
—Carl Sagan

"Okay," said Billy, closing his eyes. "I'm saying my magic words: 'Xbox,' 'TV,' 'DVR'!"

He opened his eyes and glanced around the room.

Nothing new had magically appeared. The cabin was still boring.

Billy tucked his iPhone into a pocket and headed outside.

To his left, he saw a glass-and-more-glass modern-looking house. On the right was a rambling two-story home that was kind of thrown together. One part was a castle tower, another a circus tent, and another an upside-down boat.

Billy thought the tossed-together place looked cooler than the glass house.

Strolling around to the back of the cabin, Billy noticed something weird: a giant satellite dish.

"Too bad you didn't think to hook it up to a TV," he thought out loud.

So why did Dr. Libris need a satellite dish?

Did he spend his summers trying to communicate with aliens?

Or did the big dish beam up the video feed for the worst cable TV idea in the world: The Home Security Camera Channel? *"Now you can watch empty houses filled with furniture, twenty-four hours a day, seven days a week!"*

About a hundred feet downhill from the cabin's back porch, past a picnic table and a jumble of lawn furniture, Billy could see a small red rowboat tied to a floating dock.

Way out in the middle of the lake sat an island. It was so hazy it seemed to float on the water like a bank of fog spiked with evergreen trees. The island was maybe three football fields wide and had a sheer rocky peak poking up out of the haze at its far northern edge. It looked sort of like a smooth tooth.

Billy might've stared longer (the island was kind of spooky), except he heard someone hollering at him from behind the rambling house next door.

"Hello? New neighbor? I need your help! Hurry!"

3

The little girl who'd been shouting had chocolate-colored skin, bright brown eyes, and hair knotted into three braids.

She looked like she was maybe five.

"You okay?" asked Billy.

The girl shook her head and pointed up at a tree close to the castle section of the mashed-together lake place. A baby doll in a sparkly pink dress dangled off a branch.

"I wanted to see if Dolly could fly, so I tossed her out the window," said the girl. "Can you rescue her?"

"Maybe," said Billy, leaning back to study the situation. "What's your name?"

"Billy."

"I'm Alyssa. Alyssa Andrews. We live in this house. Me, my brother Walter, and my mom and dad. Not all the time. Just for the summer. It's not really a house. It's a cottage, like the cheese? I can't climb trees. I'm only five, so it's against the rules. Walter's allowed to climb trees but he doesn't like to because trees have pollen and pollen makes his asthma worse."

"Well, don't worry. I'm pretty sure I can save Dolly."

"Really?"

"Yup. I'm twelve. I'm allowed to climb trees."

"Oh, good! Hurry!"

Billy was wiry and pretty good on the monkey bars in the playgrounds back home in the city. He figured he could handle climbing a tree. A tree was basically monkey bars made out of branches and leaves.

"Thank you!" Alyssa shouted as Billy scaled the tree.

Billy waved down at her, then cranked up a good tree-climbing tune on his iPhone. With his earbuds jammed in deep, he shinnied up higher.

And higher.

Pretty soon, he was maybe twenty feet off the ground, hugging the tree trunk tightly with his knees.

The branch that had snagged the doll wasn't thick enough to support even Billy's weight. So he stretched out his arm.

Couldn't reach the doll.

He tried again.

He stretched out his arm and his neck and was just able to nudge the doll free. It fell to the ground.

So did his iPhone.

The doll landed with a soft thud in a clump of leaves.

The iPhone that had tumbled out of Billy's pocket wasn't so lucky.

It hit a rock.

Glass crackled.

Billy slid down the tree as fast as he could and picked up his phone.

Dead.

No matter how many times he pushed the wake button or the home button or the wake and home buttons at the same time, the splintered glass remained frozen and blank.

"I'm sorry," said Alyssa.

"Is there an Apple Store around here?"

"Huh?"

"Never mind."

Billy was fixated on the sudden, horrible death of his iPhone. His mom would have to buy him a new one.

Chances of that happening? Impossible.

Because it wasn't Christmas. Or his birthday. And iPhones cost a fortune.

"Dolly wants to give you a hug," said Alyssa.

She jiggled her doll.

"That's okay," said Billy.

Alyssa narrowed her eyes. Telling her no didn't seem to be an option.

So Billy took the doll.

"There, there, there," he said, patting it on its plastic head. "Don't cry, Dolly. You're safe now."

And, of course, at that exact second, three tough-looking guys on bicycles skidded to a halt on the gravel road ten feet away.

"Awwwww. Isn't that sweet?" sneered the boy who appeared to be the bikers' leader. "Weedpole wuvs his widdle biddy baby doll."

Billy tossed the doll back to Alyssa.

The three guys—who were all about Billy's age—straddled their rides and laughed the way hyenas do when they find a wounded wildebeest.

The leader was a beefy kid dressed in a sleeveless New York Jets football jersey and bright green mesh shorts. His greasy hair was spiked up into a cockatoo Mohawk.

"That's Nick Farkas," whispered Alyssa.

"What's your name, Weedpole?" demanded Farkas.

Billy shuffled forward. "Um, uh . . . Gillfoyle," he said, trying to sound tough.

It didn't work.

"Your name is *Gillfoyle*?" Nick Farkas laughed. "What are you, a butler or something?"

"No. That's my last name. My, uh, first name is Billy."

"Um, uh," said Nick, mimicking Billy. "You sure about that, *Gillfoyle*?"

His two buddies snorted.

"What a stupid name!" said one.

"Yeah," said the other. "Stupid."

"I guess," said Billy, his eyes darting around as he looked for an escape route. He noticed something in Nick Farkas's bike basket: a stack of comic books.

"Oh, wow—you guys read *Space Lizard*? I *love* the Space Lizard."

"Well, the Space Lizard can't stand wimpy weedpoles like you," said Farkas. "In fact, he'd acid-blast your face till you shriveled up and died!"

"And then," said the guy on the left, "he'd pluck out your eyeballs with a flick of his glue-stick tongue."

"Yeah," said the other. "His tongue."

"Even though I was already dead?" asked Billy. "Isn't that a waste of glue?"

"Huh?" said Farkas.

"If I'm dead, why pluck out my eyeballs? It's not like I'm gonna feel it or, you know, go blind."

"He'd do it because the Space Lizard hates your bony butt almost as much as I do!"

Oh-kay, thought Billy. *So much for bonding over shared comic book interests.*

He figured he should just go back inside his mom's cabin and hide until summer vacation was over.

"See you later, guys," he said, waving and backing away. "Cool meeting you."

"Thanks again for saving Dolly!" shouted Alyssa.

The boys snorted some more. A broken iPhone and a pack of bullies who hated his guts? Billy wondered if it was possible for his first day at the lake to get any worse.

"I'm gonna be keeping my eye on you, Weedpole," said Farkas. "So don't you dare step across the border."

"No problem," said Billy. "Exactly which border are we talking about here?"

"The one between your lame-o cabin and my place."

Farkas jerked his thumb at the glass-on-glass box up the road.

So this was how Billy's first day and entire summer could totally get worse: Nick Farkas was his other next-door neighbor.

THE THETA PROJECT

LAB NOTE #317

Prepared by

Dr. Xiang Libris, PsyD, DLit

Subject Billy G. has moved into the test lab.

I am experiencing minor technical difficulties with the video camera located in his sleeping quarters, but otherwise, all is proceeding according to plan.

Through a bit of luck, Billy G. recently lost the use of his iPhone entertainment device. Deprived of all familiar electronic stimuli, he will soon be forced to rely solely on the cabin's book collection for his amusement.

If, as I anticipate, he passes my final aptitude test and locates the hidden key, first contact should take place in a matter of hours.

Billy had a microwaved bacon cheeseburger and a pack of peanut butter crackers for dinner.

Then he went into the living room and stared at the wall where there should've been a TV.

Billy turned and stared at a different wall.

This one had a framed black-and-white drawing of people with bulb heads walking up and down all these impossibly sideways sets of stairs or walls that faked you into thinking they were floors.

"It's an M. C. Escher print," said his mother, coming down the steps to refill her coffee mug. "He was a Dutch artist famous for his mathematically inspired woodcuts and lithographs. Dr. Libris must be a fan. There's another one just like it upstairs in my bedroom."

"People can't do what the people are doing in that picture," said Billy. "It's impossible."

His mom smiled. "Maybe. Maybe not. Some people refuse to accept the limits given to them by others."

"Huh?"

"Sorry. Guess I've been reading too many mathematical theorems supporting the concept of parallel universes. So, how are you holding up?"

"I'm fine," said Billy, following his mom into the kitchen. She was headed for the coffeepot.

"Billy, I'm sorry about your phone. But trust me—it's not the end of the world."

Easy for her to say, Billy thought. *She doesn't even text.*

"There's lots of other ways to amuse yourself up here."

"Like what?"

"Swimming. Hiking."

"It'll be dark soon."

She poured coffee into her mug and waved toward the living room. "Well, I saw some board games in those bottom cabinets."

"Cool. You want to play something?"

"Sorry. Not tonight."

Right, Billy thought. *The dissertation.*

"How about a jigsaw puzzle?" she suggested.

"Seriously? Are we at Grandma's house all of a sudden?"

She smiled at that. "Good point." She cradled her mug and headed into the living room. Billy followed her.

"Hey, have you checked out Dr. Libris's study? He has hundreds of books in there."

"Comic books?"

"Billy, what do you think kids did back before video games or TV or even electricity?"

"I don't know. Cried a lot?" He plopped down dramatically on the couch.

"No, Billy. They read books. They made up stories and games. They took nothing and turned it into something. Like your father taking a taco and turning it into a mariachi singer with a cheesy mustache."

"You like that commercial?"

"It's funny."

"But you don't like Dad."

"That's not true."

"Then why isn't he here?"

"I don't know. It's complicated." She took a breath and ran a hand through her hair.

"That's okay," said Billy, letting his mom off the hook. "I'll find something to do. You sure it's all right for me to check out Dr. Libris's study?"

"Definitely. Oh, if you want to read any of the books locked inside the bookcase, you'll need to find the key. I couldn't."

"Awesome."

Hey, a bookcase key hunt beat sitting on the couch staring at weird pictures on the walls.

Barely. But it beat it.

* * *

The door to Dr. Libris's study was heavier than any other door in the cabin.

Billy pushed it open and stepped into a pitch-dark room.

He fumbled on the wall, searching for a switch.

Found it.

A floor lamp snapped on.

Bookshelves climbed to the ceiling of the windowless room. Every inch of every shelf was crammed with books. The ceiling was covered with stamped-tin tiles.

And, of course, there was a mini security cam mounted just above the door.

Next to the floor lamp, Billy saw a leather reading chair with arms wide enough to park a cocoa mug.

On the wall behind the chair, in a narrow space between bookcases, hung a Wizard of Oz cuckoo clock with its chained pinecone weights lying sideways on the floor. Its hands stood frozen at seven and twelve.

Billy sat down in the chair and felt a small bump under his butt. He grinned.

Finding the hidden key was a cinch!

Reaching under the seat cushion, though, all he found was a switch connected to an electrical cord.

Click. Click. Nothing.

Billy was starting to think the switch was a dud when, on click three, a track of miniature spotlights lit up the far corner of the room.

"Whoa."

The darkness had been hiding the most incredible piece of furniture Billy had ever seen.

A bookcase twelve feet tall and maybe eight feet wide. It had double glass doors and a wild tangle of swirling wood carvings running along its sides, top, and bottom. There were 3-D dragons, mermaids, sea serpents, towering giants, shriveled gnomes, prancing jesters, kings, queens, soldiers, sailors, Humpty Dumpty, witches, fairies, Pinocchio, and Tiny Tim with his crutch, all chiseled delicately into the wood.

The books behind the glass doors looked pretty impressive, too. Their leather covers were a dozen different colors, their spines stamped with sparkly gold lettering.

One book was propped open on the middle shelf: *The Labors of Hercules*.

An illustration showed a muscleman wrestling a guy twice his size who looked like he might be made out of mud and rock.

Billy tugged on the brass pulls to open the doors.

The glass rattled.

Duh. His mother had told him the big bookcase was locked.

He glanced around the room, looking for a key rack. There wasn't one.

So he pushed a few of the wood carvings, hoping they might be secret buttons that would pop open the doors. He bopped a bunny on the snout. Poked a juggling bear in the belly. Tried to toggle Tiny Tim's crutch sideways.

Nothing moved. The doors were still locked.

"Okay," Billy said out loud, "if I were a zany old professor, where would I hide a key?"

He rubbed his chin and stared at the bookcase.

Then he stared some more.

Finally, he saw something. . . .

Just behind the brass keyhole, which looked like a yawning lion, Billy saw a small slip of paper the size of a fortune cookie fortune.

It was under a strip of clear plastic tape that had turned brown around the edges. The fortune itself was so tiny Billy wished he had a magnifying glass.

He looked around the room.

Some of the shelves were decorated with trinkets—like a miniature Gandalf figurine in front of a copy of *The Hobbit* and a whaling ship in a bottle near *Moby-Dick*.

But no magnifying glass.

What about Sherlock Holmes? thought Billy. *He always has that magnifying glass.*

There was a library ladder attached to the longest wall of books. Billy rolled it over a few feet, climbed up two rungs, and, working his way through the alphabet of authors, found *The Adventures of Sherlock Holmes* by Sir Arthur Conan Doyle. *Score!* Right in front of the book was a toy magnifying glass—the kind you might get with a Happy Meal. Billy wiped the layer of dust off the lens, climbed down the ladder, and went back to the bookcase.

Holding the miniature magnifier right up against the glass doors in front of the slip of paper, he squinted to read letters so small they might've been typed by a mouse:

I am an odd number.

Take away one and I become even.

What number am I?

Okay. This was pretty cool. A riddle. Billy loved solving puzzles.

He did some quick math. "Three, five, seven, and nine are odd numbers. Take away one, and you get two, four, six, and eight."

This riddle wasn't very good.

Any odd number you subtracted one from automatically turned into an even number. You didn't need to be an assistant math professor like his mom to know you could do that kind of subtraction to infinity and never end up with a decent answer.

He reread the riddle. In school, whenever he was stumped on a quiz, he found it helped to reread the question, see what it was really asking.

I am an odd number.

Take away one and I become even.

What number am I?

Billy smiled.

The riddle didn't say "subtract one." It said "take away one." *One what?* It wasn't specific.

He snapped his fingers. "The answer is seven," he said aloud. "Because if you take away one *letter*—the 's'—you end up with the word 'even.' "

Of course, knowing the answer to the riddle didn't put the bookcase key in Billy's hand.

So he climbed the library ladder again, gave himself a sideways shove, and started looking for a book with "seven" in the title.

When he reached the far end of the shelves, he stepped up a rung and gave himself a shove back the other way.

Halfway across the room, he found what he was looking for.

The Seven Voyages of Sinbad the Sailor.

Billy pulled out the book and flipped it open.

No key tumbled out.

He ruffled the pages.

They weren't bookmarked with a skinny skeleton key.

He put the book back, climbed down the ladder, and stared at the locked bookcase.

Seven *had* to be the answer to the riddle. But was it the secret to finding the key?

Billy noticed something: The brass keyhole wasn't just a yawning lion. It was the *Cowardly* Lion.

Duh!

The Wizard of Oz cuckoo clock.

The hands were frozen at seven and twelve. *Seven* o'clock.

Billy stood on the chair and examined the cuckoo clock more closely.

Were the clock hands actually keys?

Was he supposed to snap one off?

Then he had another idea.

He pried open the little door above the twelve. Something popped out.

It wasn't a cuckoo bird or even a barking Toto.

It was an antique skeleton key with the Wonderful Wizard of Oz's moon-shaped face inscribed on its head.

And it fit the bookcase's keyhole—perfectly.

THE THETA PROJECT

LAB NOTE #318

Prepared by

Dr. Xiang Libris, PsyD, DLit

My instincts proved correct.

Billy G. passed the final aptitude test. Following scant clues and using his imagination, he found the key much more quickly than I had anticipated.

Now, more than ever, I am confident that this boy will be the "key" to our extraordinary future.

Since the Hercules book was the only one in the case propped open and displayed on a book stand, Billy grabbed it first.

Inside the red, dark-as-ketchup cover, Billy found a bookplate:

Ex Libris
X. Libris

"Ex Libris X. Libris" made him smile.

His dad, who liked to play with words and had two unfinished novels and a screenplay tucked away in his desk, once told Billy that "ex libris" is Latin for "from the books of."

Dr. Libris, whose first name was Xiang, was also X. Libris.

Maybe that was why the professor collected books—just so he could have a funny-looking bookplate.

Billy sat down in the chair and skimmed a few pages of *The Labors of Hercules.*

He read about how Hercules was the strongest man in the world because he was the son of the immortal Greek god Zeus. And how his uncle, Poseidon, the god of the sea, gave Hercules's ship a poke with his trident spear to send the muscleman off on his latest adventure.

"Where's the rock dude?" Billy flipped forward past a chunk of pages.

Found him.

Hercules was in a garden where he'd just plucked three magic apples. On his way out, the big rock dude, whose name was Antaeus, challenged him to a wrestling match.

> *"You would challenge me?" said Hercules. "Do you not know who I am?"*
>
> *"I care not, you feeble fool!" roared Antaeus. "I am the mightiest wrestler who has ever lived. None can defeat me!"*
>
> *In a blind rage, Hercules grabbed Antaeus firmly around the waist, raised him high above his head, and hurled the brute to the ground.*
>
> *But Antaeus bounced back up, his strength fully restored.*
>
> *Hercules was astonished. "I do not believe my*

eyes. Not only are you not injured, your muscles have doubled in size."

"So have my skin and bones!" Antaeus flexed his rocky physique. When he stood, he was even taller than he had been when Hercules threw him to the ground.

Awesome superpower, thought Billy. He was totally getting into the story. In his mind, he could see the rocky guy growing every time Hercules knocked him down.

He could hear Antaeus roar, "You feeble fool!"

Antaeus's voice was so loud in Billy's head it made the glass in the bookcase rattle.

Wait a second.

That was impossible.

Billy looked around the room.

Nothing happened.

And then, from somewhere *outside,* far off in the distance, Billy heard Antaeus again.

"Beware, Hercules! For I shall surely crush you!"

Billy slammed the book shut.

He took a deep breath. Tried to relax.

Okay, he thought when all he could hear was his own breathing, *it was all in your head.*

He carefully creaked the book open.

"Submit to me, Hercules!"

The glass rattled again.

Billy jumped out of the reading chair. The book fell to the floor. He ran into the living room.

"Mom? Mom!"

His mother came to the landing at the top of the stairs.

"Billy? What's wrong?"

"Did you hear that?"

"Hear what?"

"A big guy. Yelling."

"I didn't hear anything. Was it one of the neighbors?"

Okay, thought Billy. *This is crazy.*

And if he told his mother that he had heard a chunky wrestler named Antaeus shouting at Hercules outside the garden of Hesperides, she'd think *he* was crazy, too!

"Uh, yeah. A neighbor. I think it might've been the kid who lives in the house next door. I met him earlier."

Suddenly, Antaeus started shouting again.

"Surrender, Hercules, you weakling! You are defeated!"

His mother didn't budge. She didn't hear a thing.

Billy, of course, did. That was why his eyeballs were practically popping out of his skull.

"Billy? Are you feeling okay?"

"Yeah, I'm fine. Maybe I'll go outside. Grab some fresh air."

"Good idea. And tomorrow you really need to eat something besides microwaved cheeseburgers and peanut butter crackers."

Billy shot her a double thumbs-up.

His mother shook her head and went back to her books.

Billy waited until she was gone. Then he bolted for the back door.

Because that was where the voices seemed to be coming from.

He noticed that the porch had the same kind of stamped-tin ceiling as Dr. Libris's study. The moon was shining bright, streaking the lake with ripples of silver.

Billy stared at the island in the distance.

All he heard were crickets. Or cicadas. Some kind of

bug rubbing its legs together. Billy was a city kid and he really didn't—

"Cursed Antaeus!"

Okay. Hercules was still alive. Now *he* was shouting, too.

"You grow bigger and uglier every time I hurl you to the ground!"

This isn't really happening, Billy told himself.

But then he saw something that changed his mind.

He was still staring at the spiky silhouette of Dr. Libris's island when, all of a sudden, one of the craggy rocks lining the shore started to move.

Started to walk.

Actually, it wasn't a rock.

When it crossed a moonlit path, Billy could clearly see the shadowy shape of a humongous man with a lumpy head and shoulders.

Antaeus.

Billy raced back to Dr. Libris's study, picked up the open Hercules book off the floor, and read what was written on the next page.

> *"You call that a kick?" cried Antaeus. "Try again, you puny little runt!"*

The cabin floor shook.

Apparently, out on the island, Hercules had kicked Antaeus and knocked him to the ground.

Billy closed the book.

The floor stopped quaking.

No one was shouting.

All Billy heard was his own rapid breathing.

He put the book back on its little easel in the bookcase.

He shut the double glass doors.

Gave the key a quick twist.

He tugged on the handles to make sure the bookcase was locked up tight.

The room remained silent.

Walking on tiptoe, Billy made his way back to the reading chair, stepped up on the cushion, and carefully re-hid the bookcase key inside the cuckoo clock.

And then he waited.

For five minutes.

Ten.

No more taunts from Antaeus or brave replies from Hercules.

No more earth-jolting body slams.

Billy ventured out to the back porch. The island was still there, of course, but no hulking wrestlers were slinking along its shoreline.

Billy couldn't figure out what the heck was going on.

It was one more riddle for him to unravel.

THE THETA PROJECT

LAB NOTE #319

Prepared by

Dr. Xiang Libris, PsyD, DLit

As predicted, our subject, Billy G., has already started interacting with the *Hercules* text. Instruments monitoring his brain functions show theta wave numbers that are off the charts. His mind is unlike any I have ever recorded.

Let us wish the boy continued good fortune on his journey. May his flights of fancy lead us all to the financial rewards we so richly deserve.

After a night of tossing and turning, fighting a lumpy pillow, and dreaming about a giant iPhone doing battle with a tub of Greek yogurt, Billy was up with the sun.

He was eager to see if he could "call up" anybody else on the island.

Making himself a bowl of cereal with a sliced banana, Billy listened for strange sounds or voices.

There weren't any.

No grunts or groans. No Hercules or Antaeus.

Because their book isn't open.

"You're up early," his mother said, coming down the stairs in her flannel bathrobe.

"Yeah," said Billy. "Wanted to get a jump on the day."

"Great. Are you running next door to talk to that boy you met yesterday?"

"No, I thought I'd do some more reading."

"You liked those books in Dr. Libris's study?"

Billy nodded. "Last night, I looked at one about Hercules. This morning, I thought I'd try something else."

"Great," said his mom. "See if he has *Robin Hood.* When I was your age, *Robin Hood* was my absolute favorite. I always imagined I was Maid Marian."

"A cleaning lady?"

His mom laughed. "No, Billy. Maid Marian is Robin Hood's girlfriend. And she was just as tough as he was."

"Cool."

"Have fun. While you're off with Robin and Marian, I'll be exploring the theoretical foundation for the existence of alternate realities—like in that M. C. Escher print with the sideways staircases."

It sounded like his mother would be lost in her own world all day, doing her math homework.

That was good. It meant Billy would be free to continue *his* research project.

Robin Hood was on the top shelf of Dr. Libris's bookcase.

Billy went to the cuckoo clock, took out the key, and slipped it back into the Cowardly Lion keyhole.

"This one's for you, Mom." He slid the emerald-green *Robin Hood* off the shelf.

He sat down in the reading chair and flipped through

the pages. He stopped at an illustration of Robin Hood and Maid Marian dueling with an evil bounty hunter who'd been hired by the even more evil Sheriff of Nottingham.

> *The bounty hunter glared savagely upon Robin and Maid Marian, both of whom were disguised as wayfaring monks. "Thou do wag thy tongues most merrily, holy friars," said the bounty hunter. "But take care, or I may cut those tongues from thy throats for thee."*

Ouch, thought Billy. *That'll hurt.*

Robin Hood and Maid Marian whipped off their monk costumes. Robin was wearing a green tunic and tights. Marian was dressed in the same thing, only her costume was brown.

> *"Thou bloody villain!" cried Robin. "Thou dare speak thusly to my fair lady?"*
>
> *"Robin Hood?" gasped the bounty hunter.*
>
> *"Ah-ha-ha-ha!" laughed Robin Hood. He flashed his bright sword in the sunlight. Maid Marian hoisted a good and heavy broadsword high above her head.*

And Billy jumped out of his seat.

Because off in the distance, he heard the clang of steel on steel.

It was happening again.

Billy glanced back at the book.

And now came the fiercest sword fight that Sherwood Forest had ever seen.

Robin Hood, Maid Marian, and the bounty hunter had launched into a three-way sword fight. And once again, it sounded like it was taking place on the island.

Carrying *Robin Hood,* Billy hurried to the back porch and read another sentence.

Up and down they fought, till all the sweet green grass was crushed by the trampling of their heels.

Billy could hear the clinking blades. The tromping of booted feet. Lots of grunting and groaning.

Then Billy heard some dialogue that couldn't be in the *Robin Hood* book.

"You dare poke at me?" roared a gravelly voice.

Great. Antaeus was back.

Somehow, even though one book was sealed up tight in the bookcase, the two books were mashing together.

Was it because Billy had read them both and now they were all mixed up in his brain?

"Mind thy manners, thou oafish ogre!" somebody with a British accent, maybe Robin Hood, shouted.

"Or we shall mind them for thee!" Another British accent. Female.

What is going on out there? Billy wondered. Then he heard another voice. Much closer.

"Hello, Billy."

No accent. It was his neighbor Alyssa.

Billy closed the *Robin Hood* book. The sounds stopped.

"What're you doing?"

"Reading."

"Really? Walter was just reading to me and guess what?"

"What?"

"It was a book about you! *The Three Billy Goats Gruff*! Get it? You're Billy, right?"

Billy just nodded. He remembered that story.

And if *The Three Billy Goats Gruff* was inside Dr. Libris's special bookcase, Billy might be able to hear a troll and a bunch of goats on the island, too.

Billy was convinced that somebody on the island was messing with his head.

He locked *Robin Hood* inside Dr. Libris's cabinet and slipped the key into his pocket.

"This has to be a gag," he said to one of the wooden pirates carved into the bookcase. "Dr. Libris probably punks people like this every summer. He rents them his cabin, then hires actors to do the voices and sound effects out on the island."

Yeah, he thought, *that would make sense.*

Except how did they know what book Billy was reading? *The TV cameras?*

Then there had been that chunky guy stomping along the shore in the dark the night before. The guy had to be at least fifteen feet tall.

How'd they swing that?

Stilts?

World's biggest marionette?

And how much would you have to pay actors to sit around all day waiting for someone to open a book?

A little after noon, Billy came to a conclusion.

He had to go explore the island.

Well, actually, he *could* just stay in Dr. Libris's cabin staring at pictures of impossibly sideways staircases and pretending nothing had ever happened.

But if he kept hearing an action-movie sound track every time he opened one of those bookcase books, he might go nutzoid.

He went into the kitchen to grab a quick lunch.

"Are you eating some fruit?" his mother called from the second floor when she heard the unmistakable crinkle of peanut butter cracker wrappers.

"Yes." Billy plucked up an apple. "And then I'm going to take the rowboat out to the island."

"Fantastic! Promise me you'll wear a life jacket?"

"I will."

"They're in the mudroom. Be careful."

"I will."

"I'll be watching out my window."

"I know."

"Billy?"

"Yes, Mom?"

"Do you know how to row a boat?"

"*Pffft*. Are you kidding? We learned it in gym class."

Okay.

That was a lie.

Billy had absolutely no idea how a rowboat worked.

Good thing there were life jackets. He might really need one.

Billy stood on the dock in the hot sun looking down at the creaky red boat as it rocked back and forth in the water.

A pair of oars was stowed in the bottom.

"What're you doing, Weedpole?"

Billy spun around.

Nick Farkas and his two evil minions were at the neighboring dock, tying off a three-person Yamaha WaveRunner Jet Ski. They must've just taken the floating motorcycle out for a spin to terrorize the trout.

"I asked you what you were doing!" shouted Farkas.

"Nothing. Just, you know. Nothing."

Farkas laughed. "Well, guess what we're doing?"

Billy wanted to say, "Learning how to use a spoon without hurting yourself?" but decided just to shrug instead.

Farkas strutted to the edge of his dock. "My mom just bought me the brand-new Space Lizard game for my Xbox."

"But wait," said one of his goons. "There's more."

"There's more," said the other.

"She also got me the cheat guide!" Farkas brandished a magazine-sized book. "So we're going inside to totally annihilate the Space Lizard. And when we're done with him, guess what we're going to do?"

Billy shrugged again. "Make Popsicle-stick pot holders?"

"No, Weedpole. We're gonna come back out here, hop on my Jet Ski, and annihilate *you*."

"We're gonna sink your dinky little boat," added his buddy.

"Yeah," said the other one. "Your boat is dinky."

Oh-kay, Billy thought. *Maybe this isn't such a good idea.*

Then, on the island, he heard Hercules shout, "By Zeus, I know not how to slay this monster!"

Farkas and his friends were already heading up to the glass house, laughing and slugging each other the whole way. If they heard the yelling, they sure didn't act like it.

Billy took a deep, steadying breath.

He had to do this thing.

He untied the docking rope from a piling and stepped down. He had one foot up on the pier and one down in the wobbly boat. He pushed his foot off the dock, shot out his arms for balance, and stood frozen like a terrified tightrope walker.

Then he moved half an inch.

And the boat nearly flipped over.

Billy dropped to his hands and knees and scrabbled around on the bottom of the boat until he was finally able to twist himself sideways and slide his butt up onto the slat of wood he was supposed to sit on to row.

Before he could slide the oars into their brackets, the boat started drifting.

Fortunately, the current carried him to the left, *away* from Nick Farkas's dock. Billy slapped at the water with one of the paddles. Unfortunately, he was turning in circles.

But then he felt something correct his course.

Something under his hull.

Something big.

Billy looked down at the lake.

Through the glassy surface of the water, he saw a huge face staring up at him.

"Aaaaah!" Billy nearly jumped out of the boat.

The man glaring up at him had long, flowing white hair and a wavy Santa Claus beard. He wore a golden starfish crown on his head and carried a humongous three-pronged spear.

He was also the size of a whale.

Billy gulped.

Because the underwater titan was Poseidon.

And he looked just like he did in the book!

Billy was frantically hanging on as Poseidon used the middle tip of his trident to nudge him toward the island. The Greek god was helping Billy exactly the way he'd helped Hercules *in the book*!

Awesome, thought Billy.

But how did Dr. Libris get the fake Greek god's spear to actually push the real rowboat?

Did the professor hire engineers from an amusement park to set this all up?

Why?

Powered by Poseidon propulsion, Billy reached the island's rocky coast in less than five minutes.

"Thanks for the assist," he said to the water.

But, of course, nobody was there.

Clenching the nylon docking line in his teeth, Billy crawled out of the rowboat. Luckily, someone had bolted a metal tie-off cleat to one of the boulders dotting the edge of the shallow lagoon.

Very convenient, Billy thought. *Probably where the ferryboat docks in the morning when it drops off all the actors and special effects technicians.*

Billy stood on the rocky shore and took in the towering row of shaggy evergreen trees ringing the island. Even though it was the middle of a hot summer day, the place seemed dark and mysterious.

He was tempted to row back to the mainland.

But he didn't.

Instead, he walked up a narrow path into the lush and sort of steamy forest. The fragrant evergreens gave way to leafier trees and thick, tangled underbrush.

Billy had hiked maybe thirty feet when he came to a wall of wire netting. Tugging at it, he realized that a massive mesh dome—like the net over the hawk cages at a zoo—covered the *entire island.*

That was why the island looked so hazy from a distance. It was under a gigantic screen lid.

Probably so they can rig ropes and pulleys off the dome, Billy thought. *To work the Rock Person puppet and stuff.*

Billy raised a loose flap cut into the netting—a doorway as wide as the path. He stepped through it and was under the dome. The narrow trail continued to wind its way into the shadowy green world. Billy followed it.

"Okay, guys," he said nervously to the trees and bushes and the actors he figured were hiding behind them. "I know you're back there. Here I come. It's showtime."

Rounding a bend, Billy came to a pair of massive wrought-iron gates set between twin columns of stacked stone.

Each of the pillars anchored a green chain-link fence that ran through the equally green undergrowth in both directions. The security fencing looked like it encircled the entire island.

The gates themselves were decorated with elaborate metal sculptures that were as amazing as the wood carvings on Dr. Libris's bookcase: a fox staring up at a cluster of grapes, a rabbit chasing a turtle, a lion with a splinter in its paw.

In the center of all the sculpted figures was a boxy black lock.

"You there! Boy!"

Billy nearly leapt out of his skin.

A strong, golden-skinned man stumbled into the

clearing on the far side of the locked gates. The guy looked like a star of the WWE or a bodybuilder who worked out sixteen hours a day.

His bulging muscles glistened with sweat. Clumps of green grass stuck out of his curly black hair and beard. His headband was tilted sideways. The lion-head-and-fur cape on his back was missing a few fangs.

Whoa, thought Billy. *Hercules.*

"Don't just stand there, boy!" cried the muscleman. "Help me!"

"Um, hi," said Billy through the bars of the gate. "You're supposed to be Hercules, right?"

"Yes. I am Hercules."

"Nice costume."

"Costume?" Hercules looked confused. "Foolish child. This is the hide of the Nemean lion that I cut off with a blade made of its own claws!"

"Riiiight. Is this a theme park? 'Fairy Tale Forest,' maybe? Did Dr. Libris hire you to trick me and my mom?"

"Please, mortal, do not speak in riddles. You are hurting the insides of my head."

"So," said Billy, looking around, "where's the big rocky guy?"

"In the name of Zeus, boy—silence! Who sent you here?"

"Poseidon."

"Poseidon? I do not understand."

"Well," Billy explained, "Poseidon shoved me across

the lake with his spear, which, by the way, is an awesome effect. Is there a chain or something under the water like on a log flume ride?"

"This is most confusing." Hercules narrowed his eyes. "What is your name, skinny mortal?"

"Billy."

"Billy? What manner of name is this?"

"I'm like the goats that are gruff."

"What? More riddles?"

"Sorry. I was making a joke. You know—*The Three Billy Goats Gruff*?"

"By Zeus, I have never met even one of these goats you speak of."

"That's because they don't really exist. But then neither do you."

"What? I am Hercules! King Eurystheus tells me what labor I must do, and I go do it. He wants me to shovel horse manure for a year, I shovel it."

"Your king sounds like a great guy. . . ."

"But I know not how to retrieve three golden apples from this garden of Hesperides."

Billy couldn't believe he was actually having this conversation.

But he was.

"Okay, first off," he said, "you're in the wrong place. This is the island of Dr. Libris, not the garden of Hesper-whatever."

Hercules wasn't listening. "The king wants the golden

apples," he continued. "Antaeus wants to stop me. I throw the brute down, he gets back up. I tackle him to the ground, he grows stronger. How might I defeat one such as this?"

"I don't know. Bullies pick on me all the time, but I've never, you know, 'defeated' one."

Just then, the earth quaked. Trees quivered. Startled birds took flight.

And a fifteen-foot-tall monster made out of rock stomped out of the forest and heaved Hercules off the ground in a bone-crushing bear hug.

Terrified, Billy grabbed the locked gate with both hands.

He was glad he was on the side without any monsters.

Antaeus had a blocky head, lumpy muscles, knobby knees, and a pleated leather chariot skirt. He looked like a rockier, browner version of the Incredible Hulk.

And it wasn't an actor on stilts or a puppet. No way.

This was real.

"I will smite you!" Antaeus bellowed as he squeezed Hercules tightly.

"Oh, the beast does grip me most mightily," gasped Hercules. "What can I do to defeat him, Billy of the goats that are gruff? Tell me! Quickly!"

Billy backed away from the gate. "I don't know!"

"Is this, then, how Hercules must meet his end? Crushed like the many I myself have crushed?"

"No, I don't think so. You still have a ton more adventures left in the book."

The rock dude squeezed Hercules tighter.

Billy's legs felt like wet noodles.

Dirt and moss were caked in the creases of Antaeus's gnarled knees. He had the earthy, stinky smell of a monkey cage.

Billy didn't think Dr. Libris's island was a secret theme park staffed by actors anymore.

He did, however, wonder if this was all some kind of major hallucination.

Maybe his mother was right.

Maybe he ate too many peanut butter crackers.

Maybe all those ingredients he'd seen on the side of the packages—junk like thiamine mononitrate and polysorbic phosphitate or whatever they put in them to make them bright orange—had totally fried his brain.

"Help me!" gasped Hercules, firmly locked in the rock man's tightening grip. "Please!"

CRUNCH!

Yow. That sounded like a bone snapping.

For half a second, Billy thought about running back down the path, jumping into his boat, and rowing home.

Maybe he could head over to Nick Farkas's house, kiss up to the head bully, and spend the rest of his summer playing *Space Lizard's Revenge*.

But Billy knew that if he ran back to the cabin, he'd never be able to read another one of Dr. Libris's books without wondering why or how they sprang to life. Plus, hallucination or not, Hercules needed help.

That was when Billy remembered he still had the bookcase key in his pocket.

Would it work on the island gates?

There was only one way to find out.

But what if the second he unlocked the gates, the blockheaded monster grabbed him, too?

Hercules yelped like a dog does when you accidentally step on its tail.

Billy sucked in as much air as his lungs could hold.

"Hercules needs my help."

(Okay, *that* was something Billy never, *ever* thought he'd hear himself say.)

He slid the bookcase key into the gate lock.

The gates sprang open.

And Billy stepped into the clearing on the other side.

“Stop!” Billy shouted at Antaeus. “That’s Hercules! Zeus is his father. You could wind up in big, big trouble. We’re talking lightning bolts, buddy!”

Suddenly, a muddy sinkhole gurgled open in front of Billy’s feet.

“Foolish mortal!” laughed the muck.

It had heaved itself up into two humps around the hole, like lips around a mouth.

Yes, now the dirt was talking to Billy, too. And it sounded like a lady.

“Too many peanut butter crackers,” said Billy. “Too many peanut butter crackers . . .”

“My son Antaeus is not afraid of Zeus, god of the skies. For Poseidon, god of the seas, is *his* father.”

“And, um, who exactly are you?” Billy asked the quivering sinkhole.

"I am Gaia! Mother Earth! Antaeus is my son."

Billy tried to sort it out in his head.

"No wonder he looks like a big walking hunk of dirt. He gets that from you. . . ."

"Indeed. And none shall defeat my son so long as he remains in my loving embrace."

"Is that why every time he hits the ground, he bounces back bigger and stronger? Is it because his mother, Mother Earth—the ground—gives him more power?"

"Hmmmm. You are wise for one so scrawny. You have discovered our family secret."

"Well," said Billy timidly, "I like to figure stuff out."

"Too bad. After my son crushes Hercules, he must crush you!"

With that, Mother Earth slammed her sludge mouth shut and vanished, leaving behind nothing but a soggy sinkhole to mark the spot where she'd appeared.

Billy's mind was racing. He had an idea.

He jammed two fingers into his mouth and whistled the way his dad had taught him to hail a taxi.

The piercing screech made Antaeus wince.

"What annoying bird makes such a squawk?" the rock man boomed, easing his grip on Hercules.

"Me," said Billy. "I, uh, just finished chatting with your, uh, mom. She wants you to give her Hercules as a Mother's Day gift."

"Huh?"

"Mother's Day! Sure, you're a little late. You really

should've given her something back in May, but, hey, you know what they say—better late than never. So just, uh, put Hercules down, and Mommy will make sure you always stay big and strong."

Antaeus did what Billy told him to.

"Quick!" Billy shouted at Hercules. "Pick him up, carry him to the shore, and toss him into the lake! But don't ever let his feet touch the ground. Touching 'Mother Earth' makes him stronger!"

Hercules stared at Billy.

"Do it!" Billy shouted.

Finally, Hercules grabbed Antaeus by the ankle, raised him off the ground, and carried him away through the forest.

"No!" Billy heard Antaeus blubber. "Put me down! Put me down!"

"As you wish!"

There was a tremendous splash.

And then everything was quiet.

Until Billy heard a rustling in the forest behind him.

Great. Now what?

"Halloa, good fellow!" cried a gallant voice. "Art thou yet another bounty hunter sent forth by the foul Sheriff of Nottingham?"

Billy spun around and saw a tall, nimble man dressed all in green. A woman dressed all in brown stepped out of the shadows behind him.

She was swinging a sword.

"If so," she said, "prepare to diest where thou do stand."

Robin Hood and Maid Marian sprang into the clearing.

Billy couldn't believe it. He was face to face with his mother's favorite fictional characters.

"What be thy name?" demanded Robin Hood, raising his bow and aiming it at Billy's chest.

"Um, Billy. You know—like the goats."

"Billy?"

"It's short for William."

"Ah-ah!" said Maid Marian, lowering her broadsword. "Thou, then, art Sir William of Goat?"

"Okay," said Billy, nodding his head, hoping Maid Marian wouldn't lop it off. "Sure. Works for me."

"Merrily, good sir," said Marian. "What brings thee to this, the secret hiding place of the most renowned outlaw in all of England?"

Billy thought for a second. "My mother sent me?"

"Thy mother?" said Robin Hood skeptically.

"You two are her favorites. She *loves* you guys!"

Robin Hood smiled. So did Maid Marian.

Then Robin took off his feathered cap, twirled it in front of his chest, and dipped into a bow.

"Sir William," said Robin, "for thy mother's sake, thou art most welcome."

"Thanks." Billy checked out the forest behind the two new characters. "So, where's that bad guy? The bounty hunter?"

"Dispatched," said Maid Marian cheerfully.

"Does that mean he's, you know, dead?"

"Ah-ha-ha-ha!" Robin Hood threw back his head and laughed heartily. "No, it means Marian scared him off with her sword."

"And I wouldst do it again," said Marian. "For the scoundrel was sent here by that vile villain the Sheriff of Nottingham."

"Aye," said Robin, squinting at the shadowy trees. "Methinks there shalt be others eager to earn the price the sheriff hath placed upon my head."

"Well, maybe, I don't know, you two should go hide in Sherwood Forest or something."

"Forsooth, I like thy notion. Come. Sherwood is over yonder."

Robin pointed.

Billy turned around.

And Hercules's field of trampled weeds had morphed

into a shady forest complete with dancing leaves, flickering sunlight, and a babbling brook. The air smelled like May and flowers. Birds chirped. A rustic log bridge spanned the rippling stream.

"Okay," said Billy. "How'd that happen?"

"Quite quickly," said Marian. "Wouldst thou not agree?"

"Yeah, but—"

Robin marched toward the narrow bridge. Marian and Billy followed him.

"The Sheriff of Nottingham will not dare to follow us hither," said Marian. "For he fears the harm that might befall him deep in the shadows of Sherwood."

"So we're safe?" asked Billy.

"Aye, marry," said Robin.

"Does that mean 'yes'?"

"Verily. Ah-ha-ha-ha!"

Suddenly, Hercules tromped out of the forest, dragging his club. He stopped at the far side of the log bridge to straighten his lion-fur cape.

"What ho!" cried Robin Hood. "Who be this lad of such might and girth?"

"He be Hercules," said Billy. "He just defeated a monster made out of rocks and mud."

Robin Hood looked impressed. "Did he indeed?"

"Well done, good sir," said Marian.

"Billy of the goats that are gruff did help me complete my quest!" Hercules shouted back. "Usually, I do not like children. They make me crazy. But Billy is different. He is bold and courageous."

"No, I'm not," said Billy. "I'm just a kid who—"

Robin snatched up a wooden staff he found on the ground near his end of the bridge.

"Robin?" said Marian. "Honestly. Must thou challenge each and every man thou meet upon the road to goodly combat?"

"Aye, marry." He called out to Hercules: "Tell me, my fine fellow—do you seek adventure this day?"

"No. I seek only to complete my twelfth—or thirteenth—labor for my king. I have lost count and am not very good with numbers."

"Well, then, what art thou good at, pray tell?" prodded Robin.

"Slaying monsters. Capturing bulls. Feats of superhuman strength."

Robin Hood placed one foot on the bridge.

"Then stand aside and let the better man pass."

"No! *You* stand aside!"

Great, thought Billy. *Now these two guys are going to fight. What kind of goofy island is this?*

Hercules and Robin Hood stormed across the log bridge and met in the middle.

"I will baste thy hide right merrily!" cried Robin.

"Ha!" laughed Hercules. "No mortal man can best me."

The two heroes started fighting on what was basically a double-wide balance beam. Robin faked like he was going to lead with his left, then whacked Hercules with his staff from the right.

Hercules didn't flinch.

He swung at Robin Hood with his club. The hit landed hard but Robin held his ground. Robin swung again. Hercules clubbed him again. Robin swung. Hercules clubbed.

Swing.

Club.

Swing.

Club.

And so it went.

For ten minutes.

Grunting and grumbling, the two men exchanged blow after blow, neither giving an inch.

"This might go on all day," said Maid Marian, setting herself down on a large rock. "It usually doth."

"Um, you guys?" Billy finally shouted. "The Sheriff of Nottingham might hear you if you keep whacking and thwacking each other like that. So maybe one of you should hurry up and fall into the river. Probably you, Robin Hood, because no way are you stronger than Hercules."

The instant Billy said this, Hercules caught Robin's oaken staff in his free hand and flipped Robin off the bridge and into the river.

"Ha! Where are you now, you boastful mortal?" said Hercules, standing triumphantly astride the bridge.

"Why, he is in the river!" cried Maid Marian, doubling over with laughter.

"I am also quite wet," Robin Hood said cheerfully. "Good sir, you didst beat me fair and square."

"Give me your hand." Hercules reached down and hauled Robin out of the stream. "You are a good fighter. My head is still buzzing from your many manly blows."

"And thou art a stouthearted lad!"

"So, um, why don't you ask him to join your band of merry men?" suggested Billy.

"Merry *people*," Marian gently corrected as she rose

off the rock. "Speak, Hercules. Wouldst thou throw in with us?"

Hercules turned to Billy. "What do you think?"

"It beats shoveling horse poop for that crazy king with the weird name."

"You are wise, little friend. Very well, Robin. Today I shall become one of your merry people!"

"And thou, Sir William of Goat?" asked Maid Marian. "Will thou join us as well?"

"Really?" said Billy. "You guys want *me*?"

Billy was sort of shocked. In gym class, nobody ever wanted him on their team.

"Please join our merry band," said Marian.

"Aye, marry," added Robin.

"Okay. Cool. I'd *love* to be on your team."

And that was when the Sheriff of Nottingham rode in on a giant black horse.

"Ah-ha!" cried the sheriff so loudly it spooked his stallion. "I have found thee!"

Robin turned to Billy and whispered, "Thou spoketh most true. Our whacking and thwacking did reveal our hiding place."

Maid Marian propped her hands on her hips and glowered at the sheriff. "You wouldst dare enter Sherwood Forest?"

"Oh, indeed I wouldst. In truth, I wouldst travel to the very ends of the earth to see you two lawless scoundrels brought to justice!"

The sheriff was a bony, sour-looking grouch dressed all in black. He sat slumped in his saddle making a face like he hadn't enjoyed whatever he'd just eaten for lunch. His horse, also completely black, was even nastier-looking—especially when it flared its enormous nostrils.

"You there! Boy!" The sheriff wagged a gloved finger at Billy. "What be thy name?"

Hercules strode forward to put his mammoth body between Billy and the sheriff, while Robin slid an arrow out of his quiver and nocked it to his bowstring. Meanwhile, Marian had her right hand hovering over her dagger.

"This is Billy of the goats that are gruff," said Hercules.

"He is known far and wide as the noble Sir William of Goat," added Robin.

"He is our new friend," said Marian.

"I see," the sheriff said with a smirk. "And didst my ears deceive me, Sir William, or didst thou just now declare thyself to be an ally to outlaws such as these?"

Billy gulped. "Maybe."

"Ah-ha-ha-ha!" laughed Robin. "Of course he did!"

The sheriff reined his horse to the left so he could prance sideways and glare at Billy.

"Take care, Sir William!" cried the sheriff. "'Tis treason to join this band of thieves. Treason, I say!"

For some reason, Billy nodded. "Okay. Thanks for the heads-up, sir."

"So you confess to being a traitor?" The sheriff swiftly pulled his sword out of its scabbard. "Then by the power vested in me by His Majesty King John, I hereby sentence thee to death!"

"Flee, Sir William!" cried Robin.

Marian whipped out her small dagger and hurled it, end over end, straight at the sheriff.

The blade hit its mark, spearing the black-hearted villain in the meaty part of his left leg.

"Curses and foul language!" the sheriff screamed as he plucked the knife out of his thigh and writhed in pain.

"Run, Billy!" shouted Hercules. "Run!"

"Take thy leave before thou diest!" added Marian.

Diest?

She didn't have to say that twice.

Billy took off like he had rockets in his shoes.

THE THETA PROJECT

LAB NOTE #320

Prepared by

Dr. Xiang Libris, PsyD, DLit

Billy G.'s first encounter with figments of his imagination did not end as well as we might have hoped.

There is a chance that a heightened sense of fear may prevent him from continuing his unsuspecting participation in our project.

Therefore, I will deliver a message to him via the pneumatic tubes installed along the edge of the lagoon.

Hopefully, it will act as the "cheese" to keep our subject racing through our maze.

Billy was totally out of breath when he reached the lagoon.

Yes, he wanted to figure out how characters from books could spring to life on the island. On the other hand, he also didn't want to "diest."

But was that even possible?

Could a make-believe sheriff chop off Billy's head with a make-believe sword?

And by the way—had Billy just rewritten literary history and turned Hercules into one of Robin Hood's merry outlaws?

Billy could see Dr. Libris's cabin in the distance. As he was about to climb into the rowboat, he noticed a bright green bottle bobbing in the water near its stern.

There was a rolled-up piece of paper tucked inside the corked bottle.

A message in a bottle?

Billy wondered if somebody in Dr. Libris's study was reading a book about shipwrecks.

He listened for the sounds of thundering hooves coming up the trail behind him.

There were none.

The Sheriff of Nottingham wasn't chasing after him.

Billy had time to see what was up with the bobbing green bottle.

He snatched it out of the water, yanked out the cork, and quickly unfurled the message, which looked like a pirate had written it:

On this island, you shall find great treasure.

Treasure?

Okay. This was extremely interesting.

Had Dr. Libris hidden some kind of treasure somewhere on his island?

If so, did the law of "finders keepers, losers weepers" apply?

Because if Billy could find the gold or jewels or winning Mega Millions Lotto cards—whatever treasure Dr. Libris had hidden on his island—he could buy himself a new iPhone. He could also pay for some of his father's silly toys and maybe get his mom a bunch of those blueberry pies she said she liked so much.

If Billy found the island's treasure, if the Gillfoyles suddenly had a ton of money, his mom and dad would have nothing to argue about, because they'd be rich!

Billy climbed into the boat and rowed as hard and as fast as he could back across the lake toward the cabin.

He thought about books that might help him on his treasure quest. Maybe *Treasure Island* by Robert Louis Stevenson or Mark Twain's *Tom Sawyer.* Billy had read *Tom Sawyer* in school. Tom and his friends were always hunting for treasure.

He'd figure out a way to deal with the sheriff, but in the meantime, he was going to need a shovel.

Since you basically row a boat backward, Billy was still facing the island as he struggled with the oars. After what felt like forever, he finally heard the sound of waves slapping against dock pilings.

"Beware!" someone shouted behind him. "I'm about to somnificate you!"

Billy twisted around and saw a kid in a polo shirt and baggy cargo shorts. The boy was standing on Dr. Libris's dock and waving his arms around like a goofy magician.

"I'm casting a slumber spell! You are sleepy, very sleepy!"

"What?"

"I'm playing my Junior Wizard card!"

"Huh?"

"It's from my Magical Battical deck!"

The boy showed Billy a crinkled card.

"Cool," said Billy. "I think some kids at my school play that game."

"Hey, did you row your boat all the way out to the island?"

"Yeah."

"That is so awesome." The boy stuffed the trading card back into his baggy pants. "I'm not very good at boat rowing. So what's your name?"

"Billy."

"Yeah. I knew that. Alyssa told me. I'm not very good at keeping secrets, either."

"Are you Alyssa's brother?"

"Yep. I'm Walter."

"Here, Walter." Billy tossed up his nylon line. "Tie me off to that post."

"Really? You want me to tie up your rowboat?"

"Yeah. On that piling."

"Okay. I'm not very good at knots but I'll give it a shot."

"Thanks," said Billy as he crawled onto the dock.

"There we go," said Walter. He had looped the nylon line around and around the pier post in a tangled jumble that ended in a sloppy shoelace-style bow. "That should hold her. I hope. So, you hungry?"

"Yeah."

Actually, Billy was starving.

"You ever been to the Red Barn?" asked Walter.

"No, but I've heard about it."

"Do you like waffle fries? Because the Red Barn's are the best." Walter reached into another cargo shorts pocket and pulled out a bright red asthma inhaler. He took two quick puffs. "So, what'd you see out on the island?"

Billy wondered how much he should tell Walter. He seemed like a pretty nice guy, but they'd only known each other for maybe two minutes.

Billy shrugged. "Nothing, really."

"I canoed out there once. Took me all day. I'm not too good with canoeing, either. Anyway, when I hiked up the path, the gate thing was locked. Dr. Libris wouldn't ever give me the key."

"You know Dr. Libris?"

"Sure. I've spent every summer up here for ten years."

Billy wondered if Walter might know a thing or two about the mysterious professor and the even more mysterious stuff happening on his island.

He also wondered if Dr. Libris had ever dropped Walter any hints about where he had hidden his treasure.

"So, where is this Red Barn?" Billy asked.

"Not too far. We can bike it."

"I don't have a bike."

"That's okay. You can borrow one of ours. We've got extra helmets, too."

"Cool. Let me run inside and tell my mom where we're going."

"Great. And when we're done with our waffle fries, I'll tell *you* all about Dr. Libris."

"Your cottage is amazing," said Billy.

"Thanks," said Walter. "My dad's an engineer. He knows how to take wacky ideas and actually make them work."

One section of the lake cottage had columns like a miniature White House; another, made out of canvas, looked like a circus tent; still another was an overturned tugboat, with the curved hull as the roof. And of course there was the thirty-foot-tall castle tower.

"My dad designed it all," Walter said proudly. "We call it the Hodgepodge Lodge. Every summer, he comes up with something new. The castle tower? He did that the year Alyssa was born, because she's his princess."

"What's he working on this year?"

"A moat."

Half a dozen bikes were leaned up against the

Hodgepodge Lodge's deck. Billy strapped on a helmet and grabbed a bike with a basket attached to the handlebars. When his mom had heard that he and Walter were heading to the Red Barn, she had given him money to pick up a blueberry pie. The basket would make bringing it home easier.

Walter and Billy hopped onto their bikes and headed for the gravel road.

The ride was extremely rickety.

"I bent my frame last week when I crashed my bike into the only car in the Red Barn parking lot," said Walter. "I'm not the world's best bicyclist."

Billy's cycling skills weren't much better than Walter's, but he kept at it.

"So," he asked when he finally felt like he wouldn't tip over, "have you ever been inside Dr. Libris's study?"

"You mean the room with the Charles Dickens bookcase?"

"What?"

"That big bookcase with all the carvings? It used to belong to Charles Dickens, the guy who wrote that book about Scrooge."

"Seriously?"

"Well, that's what Dr. Libris told me. Oh, get this—he said some of the shelves came from planks taken out of Scheherazade's trunk. She's the one who had to tell stories for a thousand and one nights and came up with 'Aladdin' on night number nine hundred and forty-two. And those carvings? They were all done by Geppetto."

"The wood-carver who created Pinocchio?"

"Yuh-huh."

"But *Pinocchio*'s just a story," said Billy. "It's not real."

"That's exactly what *I* told Dr. Libris! When I did, he shook his head and said I had 'no imagination whatsoever.' "

"That's awful."

"Yeah. Dr. Libris can be kind of crabby. That's why I never rowed out to his island except that one time. Didn't want him going all grumpy on me."

They reached Route 17.

"Stick to the shoulder," said Walter. "It's safer."

They passed a roadside stand selling fresh corn and pulled into the parking lot of a big barn-shaped building painted red.

"Guess this is the Red Barn?" said Billy.

"Yep!" said Walter, who seemed to never stop smiling. "Good name for it, huh?"

Billy grinned. He liked this guy.

They propped their bikes up against the white picket fence and went inside.

Billy and Walter shared a plate of waffle fries and then placed an order for a whole blueberry pie.

While the counter worker boxed it up, Walter nibbled on a Three Musketeers candy bar he had bought out of an old-fashioned vending machine with pull knobs.

Meanwhile, Billy studied the decorations hanging on

the Red Barn's walls—especially the photographs showing old-timey people swimming in the lake, back in the days when ladies wore swimming dresses.

Under the photos was an engraved plaque honoring Dr. Xiang Libris "for his generous donation of his private island for the creation of the Lake Katrine Bird Sanctuary."

"Is that our island?" Billy asked Walter, gesturing toward the plaque.

"Yuh-huh."

"So what's with the dome?" Billy asked. "The whole island is covered with a wire mesh net. Like a bubble over a tennis court."

"That's to stop the birds from escaping."

"So how do the birds get on the island in the first place?"

"Easy. They fly there."

"But how do they get through the net?"

Walter shrugged. "I never thought about that. I guess we could ask my dad when he gets back from Washington. He helped Dr. Libris put up the dome. Of course, Dad might not tell us anything except that it's a top-secret government project, which is what he says whenever I ask him about stuff he doesn't want to explain."

Billy thought about that for a second.

A top-secret government project?

He'd heard his mom and dad talk about the government's hiring colleges and universities to conduct classified research. Stuff for the military. A top-secret government project would also explain all the security cameras in and around the cabin, maybe the satellite dish in the backyard, too.

But what about the treasure?

Why would the government hide something valuable on the island?

Was it some kind of training exercise for army commandos?

The counter worker handed Billy a white box tied up with string.

"Enjoy."

"Thanks. Come on, Walter."

Billy was eager to hurry back to the cabin and conduct his own top-secret research project. He wanted to find out if Walter could see and hear the things Billy could see and hear whenever he read one of the books from Dr. Libris's locked bookcase.

If he was going to find the island's treasure, first he had to figure out how the crazy place worked.

Walter and Billy took a shortcut through the woods back to the lake.

They came out of the forest about one hundred yards away from Dr. Libris's cabin—but on the other side.

The side where Nick Farkas lived.

That explained why Farkas and his two beefy buddies were standing in the middle of the road, blocking it.

Billy and Walter eased on their brakes.

"Uh-oh," said Walter.

There was no way for Billy and his new friend to bike around the bully blockade.

"You know the rules, Waldo," Farkas said to Walter. "You take the shortcut through the woods, you have to give me something. Something good."

"Sure thing, Nick," said Walter. "And, might I say,

those mesh shorts look awfully comfortable. Smart choice for such a hot day."

"Shut up."

"Right." Walter wheezed and puffed on his asthma inhaler. "Something good. So, um, do you guys like wedding mints?"

"What?"

Walter showed the three thugs a fistful of pastel pink and green cubes covered with fuzzy lint.

"They had them in a bowl at the Red Barn. I find wedding mints to be both creamy and refreshing."

Farkas slapped Walter's hand hard. Mints scattered into the underbrush.

For half a second, Billy imagined a happy chipmunk bride and groom squeaking with joy: *"We have mints for our wedding! Mints for our wedding!"*

"No, Waldo," said Farkas, "we don't want your grungy, pants-crud-infested mints." He nudged his head toward Billy's bike basket. "What's in the box?"

"Pie," said Billy. "For my mom."

"Hand it over."

Billy remembered how Hercules, Robin Hood, and Maid Marian had stood up for him on the island. Maybe it was his turn.

"I'll give you the pie," he said to Farkas, "but only if you let Walter go."

"Fine." Farkas nodded at Walter. "Beat it, Waldo."

Walter looked at Billy nervously.

"It's okay," said Billy, trying his best to stay as cool as Robin Hood would. "Meet you at my place. Just knock on the door and tell my mom I'm on my way."

"Okay. Bye!"

Walter pedaled hard and wobbled away fast.

"What're you waiting for, Weedpole?" said Farkas. "Give me my pie."

"Is it blueberry?" asked one of Farkas's buddies.

"Yeah," said Billy.

"Good. That's our favorite."

"We like berries," said the other one. "Blue berries."

Behind the tough guys, Billy could see Walter dashing up the front steps of Dr. Libris's cabin. "It's my mom's favorite, too."

"So?" said Farkas. "Who gives a flying flip?"

"Me. And my mom. See, years ago, she and my dad used to drive all the way up here from New York City and—"

Farkas reached for the pie box.

Billy jerked his handlebars hard to the left. "Hang on. This is a very interesting story."

"You think I give two butt toots about your mom or your dad?"

Now Billy saw his mother come out on the porch. She and Walter shook hands and disappeared into the cabin.

"You might," said Billy, "if, you know, you ever met

her. Oh, look. There she is now." Billy tilted his head to show Farkas where to look.

Farkas and the other two took the bait and turned around.

"There's nobody—"

Billy slid his bike through the gap between the bullies.

His first few pedal pumps were so intense, gravel flew up from underneath his rear tire in a backward barrage of buckshot and pelted Farkas and his crew in the shins.

"Get back here, Weedpole!" Farkas screamed as pebbles pinged and dinged off his bare legs. "Ouch! Ooof! You're dead meat, Weedpole! You hear me? Dead. Meat."

Billy pedaled harder.

After a snack of peanut butter crackers and blueberry pie (which his mom agreed counted as a fruit, but "only for today"), Walter and Billy headed into Dr. Libris's study.

"So, Walter," said Billy, "how'd you like to go someplace you've never been before?"

"On our bikes?"

"Nope. With one of those." Billy pointed to the double glass doors.

"Those are just books, Billy."

"I don't know." Billy fished the skeleton key out of his pocket. "I think these books are special."

"Seriously?"

"Yup. That's probably why Dr. Libris keeps them locked up. And I need your help to prove it."

"Okay. So what am I doing?"

"Just pick a book. Any book."

Walter studied the shelves.

"How about *The Hunchback of Notre Dame*? They have a good football team. Or maybe *20,000 Leagues Under the Sea*. *Pollyanna* looks interesting, too. . . ."

Billy realized this could go on all day. "How about *The Three Musketeers*?" he suggested.

"Excellent. They make a very delicious candy bar."

"Great. Okay—sit in that chair."

"Right." Walter sat down. "Now what?"

"Read."

"From the beginning?"

"Doesn't matter. Just pick a page and start."

"What're you going to do?" Walter asked, looking up at Billy.

"Wait."

"Really? Why?"

"It's all part of the experiment."

"Gotcha. Okay. Here I go. I'm going to start reading."

"Great." Billy walked back to the bookcase.

"*The Three Musketeers*," said Walter, reading the cover out loud. "Here I go. Picking a page."

"Walter?"

"Yeah, Billy?"

"Just read, okay?"

"Right."

And finally, Walter started reading. Silently, thank goodness. For ten whole minutes he read his book without saying a word.

Billy spent that same ten minutes straining his ears, listening for any strange voices or unusual sounds.

"Okay," said Walter. "Now what?"

"Did you hear anything?" asked Billy.

"Nope."

"Voices?"

"Nope."

"Sound effects?"

"Nope."

"Were there any in the story?"

"Oh, yeah. Lots." Walter handed Billy the book. Billy skimmed the page.

Cardinal Richelieu's guards were threatening the three musketeers—Athos, Porthos, and Aramis—plus a young guy named D'Artagnan, who wanted to become one of the king's musketeers. Swords were about to start clanking.

> *"What have you decided?" cried the captain of the Cardinal's guards.*
>
> *"That we four are about to have the honor of attacking you," replied Aramis, lifting his hat with one hand while drawing his sword with the other.*
>
> *The combatants rushed upon each other with a great fury.*

Billy looked up from the book. In the distance he could hear the *WHISH-CLINK-CHINK* of fencing foils smacking into each other.

Then he heard voices, rich with thick French accents.

"Touché!"

"En garde!"

Billy turned to Walter, who was fidgeting with a pocket on his cargo shorts.

"You don't hear that?"

Walter tilted his head. "Hold on. Wait a second. Okay. I hear it."

"You do?"

"Yep. It's a bird. Maybe a chickadee."

Billy wondered, once again, if he was just imagining all this. Was he going crazy?

Billy needed to take Walter out to the island to see if he saw any of the stuff Billy had seen (or *thought* he'd seen).

Of course, it could be dangerous.

After all, the Sheriff of Nottingham was probably still l[illegible]ng around out there. They could both "diest."

Then again, if Billy didn't figure this thing out, his brain might explodeth.

He might also blow his shot at finding the treasure.

"So, Walter," he said, "what if I told you that this bookcase key also opens the gate out on the island?"

"Then what're we waiting for? Let's go!" Walter raced out of the cabin and down the hill to the dock. Billy laughed and took off after him.

22

Without Poseidon's help, it took about twenty sweaty minutes for Billy and Walter to row to the sheltered cove on the southern tip of the island.

The bobbing green bottle was gone, but Billy still had its message tucked in his pocket.

"Follow me." Billy hiked up the trail. Walter hiked after him.

When they reached the dome flap, Billy flipped it up. The two boys stepped in and followed the path further into the forest. Billy could hear the frenzied clatter of dueling swords.

Walter slowed down. His ears perked up.

"Billy? Is this island like a sword-fighting camp?"

Billy could barely contain his excitement. "You hear that?" *Finally!*

"Yeah," said Walter. "So that's why there's a locked

gate. Does the bird sanctuary double as the top-secret training grounds for the U.S. Olympic fencing team?"

"Actually, I think these guys are from France."

"Adieu!" shouted one of the musketeers. "Run, you cowards. Run!"

"Run back to Cardinal Richelieu," cried another, "and tell him that you have tasted the king's steel!"

"Well played, Monsieur D'Artagnan," said the third musketeer. "We could not have won this victory without you. Therefore, I will now kiss you tenderly upon both of the cheeks! *Mmwah! Mmwah!*"

"Wait a second," said Walter. "D'Artagnan was the name of a guy in that book we were just reading."

"Yup," said Billy with a smile. "Welcome to the island of Dr. Libris!"

They dashed up the trail to the gate.

The clearing on the other side wasn't a muddy field or Sherwood Forest anymore. It looked like a cobblestone square from old-time France. There was a signpost reading *"Bienvenue à Paris."*

Billy unlocked the gate.

The three musketeers and their young recruit, D'Artagnan, were drinking from metal mugs at an outdoor cafe, quenching their thirst after their duel with Cardinal Richelieu's guards. All four men had long, curly hair flowing from under their feathered hats. They sported tiny chin beards and thin mustaches. They wore knee-high boots, baggy balloon pants, and short red coats, emblazoned with a royal coat of arms, that hung over their shoulders like sleeveless ponchos.

And, of course, they all had swords belted to their hips.

"May I refill your tankard, Aramis?" said the musketeer with the biggest belly.

"No, thank you, Porthos. I must not ruin my exquisite physique."

Porthos turned to the oldest musketeer. "And you, Athos?"

"No. I do not care for this beverage. Somehow, it makes me sad."

"Billy?" Walter whispered. "Who are those guys? And why does that sign say 'Paris' when we're in the middle of Lake Katrine?"

"You ready to meet your heroes?" Billy asked Walter.

"Huh?"

"You love their candy bar," said Billy, squeaking open the gate. "Now it's time to meet the men it was named after!"

"Whoa! One of those guys is Snickers? No, wait. Twix?"

"Walter? It's the three musketeers!"

"Nuh-unh. There's four of them."

"Sure, if you count D'Artagnan. He's not actually a musketeer. Not yet. But he wants to be."

"Really?"

"Yup. It's just like in the book."

THE THETA PROJECT

LAB NOTE #321

Prepared by

Dr. Xiang Libris, PsyD, DLit

The promise of "treasure" has proven quite effective in luring Billy G. back to the island.

Our subject has also become friendly with another boy, Walter A., who has been my neighbor on the shores of Lake Katrine for ten summers.

Under the dome, Walter A. can see and hear the characters generated by Billy G.'s imaginings.

This interaction between the two boys solidifies my theory that theta waves can be harvested to produce very real results.

In other words, we are one step closer to making money.

23

The three musketeers and D'Artagnan leaned back in their café chairs.

The melancholy older guy, Athos, propped his boots up on a barrel. The one who thought he was handsome, Aramis, studied his reflection in the side of his shiny mug. Porthos belched. D'Artagnan fumed.

"Come on," Billy said to Walter. "I'll show you how it works."

Billy strolled across the cobblestone Parisian square. Walter followed him.

Then Billy made a big mistake.

He smiled.

D'Artagnan leapt out of his chair. One hand went to the hilt of his sword, the other to his hip. "You dare to insult *moi*?"

"No," said Billy. "Sorry."

"You must forgive D'Artagnan," said Athos. "He takes every smile for an insult."

"What is your name, boy?" asked Porthos, chomping off the end of a long loaf of bread.

"I'm Billy. And this is my friend Walter."

Aramis squinted at the two boys. "Tell me: Be you for the cardinal or the king?"

"Mind you, think before you answer," offered Athos. "For we have all sworn allegiance to the king."

"Well, uh, this is America," said Billy. "We don't really have kings."

"But," added Walter, "this island is a bird sanctuary. So you might see some cardinals."

All the musketeers leapt to their feet, their hands going to their hips and their swords.

"That was a joke," Billy said quickly. "Heh-heh-heh."

"You dare insult us once more with your laughter?" cried D'Artagnan. In a flash, he drew out his rapier, and after a few fancy swishes and swirls, he placed it in front of his face.

"*En garde!* I challenge you both to a duel!"

"B-B-Billy?" stammered Walter. "These guys are actors, right? And this scenery, it's fake. Right?"

"I don't think so."

"All for one!" shouted Aramis.

"And one for all!" replied the others.

The musketeers raised and touched their four swords.

Walter wheezed.

"Use your inhaler," said Billy.

Maybe coming back to the island wasn't such a great idea, he thought. Yes, there might be treasure, but there were definitely swords.

And arrows!

A shaft whizzed through the air. It landed with a tail-twanging *thunk* in a wooden keg. A purple geyser gushed out around the arrowhead.

Robin Hood and Maid Marian sprang from the shadows, their bowstrings pulled taut.

Hercules, now wearing tight green leggings, a green tunic bursting at the seams, and a green cap two sizes too small, trudged in behind them, swinging his cudgel.

"Fear not, good Sir William!" cried Robin. "We shall protect thee!"

"Aye," said Maid Marian, aiming her arrow at Porthos's belly. "For the portly one doth make a most excellent target."

Walter tugged on Billy's sleeve. "Are these guys friends of yours?"

Billy grinned. How cool was this? Some of the most famous characters ever were now his buds.

"Yeah," he said modestly. "We met the last time I rowed out here."

"You *imbéciles*!" shouted Porthos, staring down at the leaking barrel. "What have you done to my liquid refreshment?"

"What we shall soon do to thee!" laughed Robin.

"Now then," said Maid Marian, pulling out a burlap sack, "if thou love thy lives, kindly give up all of thy gold!"

"You would dare to rob us?" demanded D'Artagnan.

"Indeed we would!" said Robin.

"We are merry people," added Hercules. "We rob from the rich and pour it on the floor."

"No," said Robin. "We rob from the rich and *give* to the *poor*."

Hercules nodded. "Right. Got it. Sorry."

"Silence!" D'Artagnan said, seething. "Prepare to die!"

Flaring swords, aiming arrows, and swinging clubs, the seven fictional characters circled each other.

Billy and Walter ended up in the center of that circle.

"Oh, man," said Walter. "Billy? Those weapons look super realistic. . . ."

"Hang on," said Billy. "Let me think. There has to be a way out of this. . . ."

"We need the Junior Wizard."

Billy was confused. "What? Who?"

"The Junior Wizard." Walter yanked the trading card out of his pants pocket. "We need to somnificate these guys."

"What?"

Walter flipped over the card and read what was printed on the back. " 'The Junior Wizard can cast a level-four slumber spell if he has collected enough snoozle powder.' "

Suddenly, a spry little man in a star-spangled robe and wizard hat appeared in the square and started wildly waving a wand.

"Wow!" said Walter. "It's him. It's really him! How'd I do that?"

"I don't know," said Billy. "Honestly. I don't know how any of this works!"

Especially now that Walter had conjured up a character who wasn't even from a book, let alone a book from Dr. Libris's special bookcase.

The Junior Wizard reached into his twinkling robe and flung up a fistful of golden glitter.

As it fluttered down, Hercules yawned. "Oh, me. My club feels so heavy."

"My bow and arrow, too," added Maid Marian, rubbing her sleepy eyes.

"Ah-ha-ha-ha," mumbled Robin drowsily.

"I fear I ate too much," said Porthos, dropping his sword and stretching like a cat. "I need a quick nap."

The other musketeers' swords clinked, plinked, and clanked on the cobblestones. They all (except Billy and Walter) slumped to their knees, toppled forward, and fell fast asleep.

The Junior Wizard smiled, bowed, and disappeared.

"Wow," said Billy. "That's a pretty incredible card."

"Yeah," said Walter. "I am *so* glad I traded for it."

"Any idea how long they'll be asleep?"

"Don't worry. It's a level-four spell."

Billy nodded as if he understood what that meant. "You know what I'm thinking?"

"Yeah," said Walter. "Me too."

"Let's get out of here!"

Neither Billy nor Walter said anything for a very long time as they rowed back to the mainland.

And then Walter exploded.

"Okay—what was all that? The three musketeers, Hercules, Robin Hood, Maid Marian, *and* the Junior Wizard? Did I miss anybody?"

"D'Artagnan," said Billy. "He was there, too."

"Right. The *fourth* musketeer."

"And yesterday Hercules was wrestling a rock man, Poseidon was swimming around the island, and Mother Earth talked to me through a sinkhole."

"There was a rock man?"

"Yeah."

"Billy?"

"Yeah?"

"This is ridiculous."

"Tell me about it. But since we could both see and hear it once we were on the island, I think it's real."

"Wait a second. Could you see and hear stuff *before* we stepped under the dome?"

"If I am in Dr. Libris's study, I can hear things. If I'm out on the back porch, I can see things, too. I thought it was all somehow coming from the books in Dr. Libris's special bookcase."

"But the Junior Wizard didn't come from one of Dr. Libris's special books. He came from my deck of Magical Battical cards."

"I know. It doesn't make sense."

Billy kept working the oars. The boat kept sliding across the lake. The two boys kept quietly trying to figure out what the heck was going on.

"Wait a second," said Walter. "Dr. Libris is a professor, right?"

Billy nodded. "At the college where my mom works. It's how come we were able to rent his cabin. Of course, we had to go to his office to meet him first. Actually, my mom is the only one who *met* Dr. Libris. I just had to take a test."

"A college test?"

"It was just a bunch of ink blots. To keep me busy while Mom talked to Dr. Libris, they showed me these black blobs and I had to write down what I saw. One sort of reminded me of a dinosaur juggling spaghetti. Another one I said was a bunny rabbit playing linebacker for the Pittsburgh Steelers."

"But why did Dr. Libris give you a test?"

"I think he was really testing to see if I would chuck the ink blots and start messing up his waiting room. He probably wanted to see if I was the kind of kid who'd trash his cabin if he rented it to my mom. So, since the camera was watching, I played along. Wrote up descriptions for a dozen different squiggles."

"There was a camera?"

"Yup. Dr. Libris loves security cameras. Has them all over his cabin, too."

"Well, *maybe,*" said Walter, "Dr. Libris is doing some kind of research project for the college's English department to encourage kids to read. So he uses all those cameras in the cabin to see what book you're reading, and then someone tells the actors out on the island what costumes they need to put on to make the story come to life for you."

"But the Junior Wizard showed up like two seconds after you read his card. And don't forget: Yesterday, I was ten feet away from a monster made out of mud and rocks. They're not actors, Walter. I thought the same thing at first. Now I think it's like that Escher print hanging on the wall in Dr. Libris's cabin, the one with the sideways staircases. It seems impossible, it looks impossible, and it probably should be impossible, but somehow it just isn't."

Walter and Billy thought about that for a few minutes

as they drifted across the lake. The sun was starting to set.

"I guess it could be a parallel universe," mumbled Billy.

Walter nodded. "I've heard about those."

"My mom's writing her dissertation about 'em. She told me that in a parallel universe, things turn out differently than they do here. Animals that are extinct in our world might still be alive in a parallel world."

"Like dinosaurs?"

"It's possible."

"Awesome. Tell your mom I can't wait to read her dissertation. Especially the part about the dinosaurs."

"Will do," said Billy as he tugged on the oars.

"I have another idea, too," said Walter.

"What?"

"This is all a dream and we're both asleep right now."

That made Billy laugh.

"So," said Walter, "do you want to go home and pretend none of this ever happened?"

"Really?"

"It's an option. I'm just putting it out there."

Billy looked at Walter with a mischievous grin. "Quit now? And pass up a once-in-a-lifetime chance to go on adventures with the greatest characters of all time?"

"Well, when you say it like that . . ."

Billy decided it was time to let Walter in on his other big secret.

"Besides, we may need their help," he said cryptically.

"Help? For what?"

Billy showed Walter the crinkled message from the bobbing green bottle.

On this island, you shall find great treasure.

"Okay," said Walter as he dragged a shovel into Billy's yard the next morning. "I figured it out."

"You did?" said Billy.

"Yuh-huh. It's a black hole."

"Like in space?"

"Exactly. Only this is the first one ever discovered on the planet Earth."

"I don't know, Walter."

"Think about it, Billy. Black holes are portals to parallel universes like in your mom's dissertation. Plus, a parallel universe would be the perfect place to hide treasure, because no one could find it unless they found your black hole first."

"But black holes have so much gravity, nothing, not even light, can escape. We wouldn't be able to go in and come out the same way."

"Oh," said Walter. "Right. Forgot about that. Guess I'm not very good at astronomy, either. Okay, skip the black hole. Let's go find that treasure."

Billy grinned. "Come inside. I think I found us the perfect treasure-hunting partner."

Billy led Walter into Dr. Libris's study.

"Hey, Billy, you ever notice that the ceiling tiles in here are made out of metal?"

"Yeah. Tin. The same kind are on the ceiling over the back porch, too."

"My dad says tin is a good conductor of electricity," said Walter.

"Huh," said Billy. "And have you noticed—there's a satellite dish in the backyard but no TV in the cabin?"

"So *maybe* . . . the tin ceiling picks up your electronic brain signals when you read a book and transmits them to the satellite dish, which beams them up to space, where they hit a satellite with a bunch of digital movie projectors that send holographic images down to the island or directly to the underwater cable my dad's construction crew ran out there a couple years ago."

"Whoa," said Billy. "Wait a second. They ran a cable out to the island?"

"Yuh-huh. They spooled it off the back of a big boat. My dad said it was for the bird sanctuary's telecommunications and Internet system. I asked him if birds use landline phones and Web browsers. He told me that information was classified."

Billy thought about his encounter with Poseidon. Walter's underwater cable might explain that.

"Uh-oh," said Walter, studying the books lined up in the case. "Stay away from that one." He was pointing at *The Time Machine* by H. G. Wells. "We have enough weirdness already. You definitely don't want to mess with the space-time continuum, too."

"Good point."

"You should pick *Treasure Island*. Get it? Island? Treasure? *Treasure Island!*"

"I had the same idea," said Billy. "But there's no *Treasure Island* on any of the shelves."

"No *Treasure Island*?" Walter sounded bummed.

"Nope. So I started thinking about other books with treasure or treasure hunters in them."

Walter snapped his fingers. "*National Treasure Two: Book of Secrets*! *Raiders of the Lost Ark*!"

"Those are movies, Walter."

"Weren't they books first?"

"Nope. Sorry." Billy opened up the bookcase and took out a midnight-blue clothbound edition of *The Adventures of Tom Sawyer* by Mark Twain. "But Tom Sawyer goes treasure hunting all the time. He's an expert. He can tell us where to start digging."

"So we don't waste a lot of time digging random holes like in that other book!"

"*Holes,*" said Billy.

"Yeah. That one."

Billy sat down in the comfy chair, flipped open *Tom Sawyer,* and started reading.

> *Tom lay awake and waited, in restless impatience. When it seemed to him that it must be nearly daylight, he heard the clock strike ten!*

In the distance, Billy heard a clock tolling ten times.

"Did you hear that?" he asked Walter in an anxious whisper.

"Nope."

Same as the day before. Billy heard stuff in the study; Walter didn't.

"Okay," he said. "Here come the meows."

"Is there a cat in the book?" asked Walter.

"Nope. It's Tom Sawyer calling out to his friends because he's ready to go treasure hunting. And you know what? So am I!"

Billy ran out the door first.

"I'm right behind you!" cried Walter.

Billy manned the oars, and fifteen minutes later they reached the island.

Walter tied off their docking line with another messy shambles of a knot. Then the two boys toted their shovels up the mulched path, ready to strike it rich.

"Let's hope all those characters from yesterday are still asleep," said Walter.

"Well, you said it was a level-four spell. That ought to keep them conked out. Right?"

Walter nodded. "Definitely. I think."

Billy held open the dome flap so Walter could step in ahead of him.

"Walter?" said Billy.

"Yeah?"

Billy pointed at Walter's butt. "What's that?"

"What's what?"

"The rectangle jammed down the back of your pants."

"Oh," said Walter nervously. "Nothing. I just grabbed some fresh reading material."

"What?"

"It's a book from the bookcase."

Billy was confused. "But I brought *Tom Sawyer.*"

"I know," said Walter. "But seeing the Junior Wizard come to life was so cool I wanted to try it again."

"But . . ."

"Don't worry, Billy. I picked something totally safe." Walter pulled out the book and showed it to Billy. "It's called *Pollyanna: The Glad Book*. Judging from her picture, I don't think this Pollyanna girl will be armed or dangerous like all those people yesterday."

On the cover of the new book, Billy saw a happy girl in a straw hat and pigtails toting a basket of flowers.

"Fine," said Billy. "Who knows? Maybe Pollyanna is a treasure hunter, too."

"I don't think so," said Walter, flipping through some pages. "So far, she's mostly just 'glad, glad, glad' about *everything.*"

"Well, listen to this," said Billy as he riffled through the pages of *Tom Sawyer.* "It's from Chapter Sixteen. They're on a sandbar in the river and Tom says, 'I bet there's been pirates on this island before, boys. They've hid treasures here somewhere. How'd you feel to light on a rotten chest full of gold and silver—hey?' "

"I'd feel awesome!" said Walter.

The two boys raced up the trail with their shovels but stopped in their tracks when they reached the gate.

Paris was gone.

So were Robin Hood, Maid Marian, Hercules, and all four of the musketeers.

The cobblestone Parisian square was now a wide country lane lined with tall elm trees.

Walter pulled his rubber-banded stack of trading cards out of his shorts, found the Junior Wizard, and started reading a grid of power stats on the back.

"Oops," he said. "Guess I'm not very good at playing Magical Battical, either."

"What?"

"I forgot. Level-four spells only last one turn."

"How long is a turn?"

"Depends. Usually about an hour."

Billy sighed and unlocked the gate. "Let's go find 'em."

Walter propped the shovels up against one of the twin stone columns.

The two friends headed up the shady country lane.

But they didn't walk very far.

Because they saw something nailed to one of the elms lining the path.

A WANTED poster—with Billy's name on it.

WANTED
DEAD OR ALIVE
ROBIN HOOD
&
SIR WILLIAM OF GOAT,
HE WHO DIDST CAUSE ME
TO BE CRIPPLED
—THE SHERIFF OF NOTTINGHAM

"This isn't good," said Billy.

He and Walter walked up the road a few more yards. The next elm tree had a WANTED poster nailed to it, too.

And so did all the other elms lining both sides of the road.

"Excuse me," cried a happy voice, "but why do you two boys look so glum? Especially since today is such a bright and cheery day!"

"No, it's not," said Billy.

"Well, you can make it better! Just play the glad game!"

"Woo-hoo!" said Walter with an excited arm pump. "I did it again! That's her! That's Pollyanna."

The girl smiling at Billy and Walter was maybe eleven years old with lots of freckles, two blond pigtails, and a straw hat the size of a small umbrella. She wore a bell-shaped yellow gingham dress that made her look like an upside-down daffodil. She also carried a basket of freshly cut yellow flowers. Daffodils.

"What's the glad game?" asked Billy.

"Oh, it's ever so simple," gushed Pollyanna. "Change a few words and you can change everything! My father and I started playing it when I asked for a doll and got crutches instead. The game was to find something to be glad about in everything."

"Even crutches?" said Walter.

"Of course, goosey! Why, just be glad because you don't need them."

"Well," said Billy, "I'd be really glad if my name wasn't on that 'wanted' poster."

"But I think it's wonderful!" said Pollyanna, sort of dancing on her toes.

"You do?"

"Why, you're nearly as famous as Robin Hood, and, heavens—he's legendary."

"Do you know Robin Hood?" asked Billy.

"Oh, yes!"

"Any idea where he might be? We're kind of looking for him."

"I gather he and his merry people are on their way to the Saint Petersburg Sunday School Picnic and Archery Contest."

"Saint Petersburg?" asked Walter. "Where's that?"

"Just up the road a piece in Missouri, right on the banks of the Mississippi River."

Pollyanna reached into her flower basket and pulled out a parchment scroll.

"Mr. Hood was kind enough to give me this handbill announcing today's event."

She passed the small scroll to Walter.

"Huh," said Walter. " 'Ye Olde-Fashioned Sunday School Picnic and Archery Contest. Today. Saint Petersburg, Missouri.' " He looked up at Billy. "The grand prize is an arrow made out of solid gold. Robin Hood will win it for sure."

Something didn't feel right. Billy shook his head. "It's a trap."

"Heavens," said Pollyanna. "Whatever do you mean?"

"The Sheriff of Nottingham knows Robin can't resist an archery contest with a prize like that. So when he shows up at the Sunday school picnic, the sheriff will arrest him. He'd probably like to arrest me, too."

"Billy?" said Walter. "Why is the sheriff after you?"

"He thinks I'm a traitor."

"How come?"

"I sort of said I was joining Robin Hood's merry band of outlaws."

"Maybe we should go home," said Walter. "We could come back tomorrow to find the treasure."

"We can't, Walter. Robin Hood's in danger. Maid Marian and Hercules, too. And it's my fault. Maid Marian only threw her dagger at the sheriff to protect me." Billy turned to Pollyanna. "Can you take us to the picnic?"

"I'd be glad to show you boys the way."

"Wait," said Walter. "What if the sheriff *does* arrest you? What'll you do?"

Billy shrugged. "I don't know. I guess I'll play Pollyanna's glad game."

Pollyanna clapped her hands. "Oh, goody!" She skipped up the trail.

Billy and Walter followed her.

Neither one was skipping.

The winding path ended in a lush green glen filled with tables, tents, and fluttering banners.

The people strolling across the grass and working in the canvas booths were dressed in their Sunday best and looked like they had stepped out of an old-fashioned photograph taken before the Civil War.

The fluttering banners, on the other hand, came from some other century—maybe the Middle Ages.

"Golly," said Pollyanna. "I'm so glad we're here! Now, if you two will excuse me, I need to go help out over in the pie tent."

"There's pie?" said Walter.

"Of course, goosey. You can't have a proper picnic without pie."

A barefoot boy munching on an apple sauntered toward Billy, Walter, and Pollyanna. He was wearing blue jeans cut off at the knee, a faded blue shirt, and leather suspenders, and he was crowned with a speckled straw hat.

"Hello, Thomas Sawyer," said Pollyanna.

"Thomas?" said the boy. "That's the name they lick me by. I'm 'Tom' when I'm good."

"Well, then—see you later, *Tom*!" Pollyanna pranced off to her pie pavilion.

"Hi, Tom," said Walter. "I'm Walter. This is my friend Billy. We're here to hunt for treasure."

"I figured you weren't here to cure warts with spunk-water. Did you boys bring shovels?"

Walter nodded eagerly. "Yeah. Two of 'em. We left them back at the gate."

"Wait," said Billy. "First we need to rescue Robin Hood."

"You two playing Robin Hood?" said Tom Sawyer. "Me and Joe Harper play Robin Hood all the time. Why, I'd rather be an outlaw in Sherwood Forest than president of the United States."

"Not me."

Behind Tom Sawyer, Billy had just seen the Sheriff of Nottingham limp his way up a set of steps to a raised platform. Four stern deputies marched behind him.

"Uh-oh," said Billy. "It's the musketeers. Looks like they're working for the sheriff now."

"Why, that ain't right," said Tom Sawyer. "That ain't the way it is in the book."

Billy didn't have time to explain to Tom Sawyer how the three musketeers had ended up in *Robin Hood*.

He and Walter slipped behind an oak tree to hide. Tom hid with them. The three boys were close enough to hear the sheriff as he gave orders to the musketeers.

"A right good reward have I offered to whosoever should bring me Robin Hood and the traitorous Sir William of Goat. But no man in Missouri hath proved brave enough. Therefore, brave musketeers, keep an eye upon our contestants. Unless Robin Hood should prove a coward as well as a rogue, he will surely be amongst the archers competing here this day."

"Wait with Tom," Billy said to Walter. "I need to go warn Robin and Hercules."

"Hercules?" said Tom Sawyer. "Is he here, too?"

"See that archer in the hooded robe? The huge guy disguised as a monk?"

"That there is Hercules?"

"Yup."

"Oh, this is bully!" exclaimed Tom.

"Does 'bully' mean 'good'?" asked Walter.

"Nope," said Tom. "Bully is better than good."

"Well, this isn't 'bully,'" said Billy. "The sheriff wants to hang us all."

"Don't let him see your face," suggested Walter.

"Good idea. Can I borrow your hat, Tom?"

"I reckon so."

Billy put on Tom's straw hat, lowered his head, and trotted away from the tree. He had to talk to Hercules, warn him about the danger.

Behind him, someone blew a flourish of trumpet blasts.

The archery contest was about to begin.

Billy needed to hurry.

"Herc!" Billy whispered when he reached the big man.

"Billy?" said Hercules. "What are you doing here?"

"You guys are in trouble. Where's Robin?"

Hercules nodded toward an archer at the far end of the shooting line. The guy was dressed in tattered clothes and a feathered cap, and he wore a black patch over one eye. Despite the disguise, Billy knew the half-blind beggar was really Robin Hood.

"Is Maid Marian here?"

"No," said Hercules. "Robin said too many royals would come to this picnic and they'd all recognize her, since her father is Sir Richard of Leaford."

Great, thought Billy. *If things get ugly, it will just be Hercules and his bow against the four musketeers' swords.*

"This is a trap," said Billy. "The sheriff is going to arrest Robin the second he shoots his winning arrow."

"Fear not, for I shall protect him." Hercules nocked an arrow and tugged back with all his might.

The bow snapped.

"By Zeus," he muttered, "that is the fourth bow I have broken this day."

The trumpet sounded again and all the archers in the line stepped forward to take their shots.

Arrows sliced through the air. One archer hit the dead center of his hay-bale target's bull's-eye.

"We have a winner!" cried the Sheriff of Nottingham.

"Nay," said the half-blind beggar. "For I have not yet loosed my shaft."

He aimed his arrow at the very same target.

"Are you blind in both eyes, you tangle-headed old fool?" cried the champion archer. "How could you top my shot?"

"Top it, I cannot. But split it, sir, I might."

Billy ducked his head again and hurried down the line of archers, using their bodies as a shield so the sheriff couldn't see him.

"Robin? It's me. Sir William. The Sheriff of Nottingham has the musketeers on his team. They're going to arrest us both."

"Ah-ha-ha-ha!" Robin laughed merrily. "Fear not, Sir William, for the day belongs to the brave."

Robin raised his elbow, drew back his bowstring, and shot an arrow that shredded the other archer's shaft into two splintered halves. Double bull's-eye.

The crowd cheered.

"You there!" called the sheriff. "Come, noble archer, claim thy prize. For well and fairly hast thou won it."

Tucking his chin to his chest, hiding under the brim of Tom Sawyer's hat, Billy followed Robin as he proudly marched to the sheriff's reviewing stand.

But when Robin held out his hand to accept his trophy, the sheriff plucked the golden arrow out of his reach.

"Before thou claimeth thy prize, good sir, tell me—art thou not that cowardly knave known high and low as Robin Hood?"

"Robin's not a coward!" shouted Hercules, tearing off his robe to reveal his tight green tunic and leggings.

Now Robin threw off his disguise, too. "And I shall dash to pieces any who dare say that I am!"

"Ah-ha!" shouted the sheriff. "Seize him! Seize Robin Hood!"

The musketeers drew their swords.

"All for one, and one for—"

Hercules grabbed the nearest tent pole, which made the canvas collapse.

"By Zeus," cried Hercules, "I will smite *all* of you!"

He swung the pointy-tipped post like a mighty baseball bat and knocked the four swords out of the musketeers' hands with one swoop.

"Ah-ha-ha-ha!" laughed Robin. "There shall be no smiting here today, my good friend." He snatched the golden arrow from the terrified sheriff. "But mark my words,

Sheriff: Shouldst thou ever attempt to trap me again, Hercules shall knock thy noggin into the next county. Come, good friend. Let us flee!"

"Follow me to my cave, boys!" shouted Tom Sawyer. "It's a bully hiding place!"

"Huzzah!" cried Robin.

"Hey nonny-nonny!" added Hercules.

Tom Sawyer raced across the meadow and headed toward the craggy mountain on the horizon. Robin Hood and Hercules raced after him.

Billy and Walter were all alone.

Except, of course, for the Sheriff of Nottingham and the four musketeers.

"Chase after those scoundrels!" cried the sheriff. "Seize them!"

The four swashbucklers leapt off the platform to collect their fallen weapons.

They were only ten feet away from Billy and Walter.

"Wait!" yelled Billy, hoping to buy his friends a little time. He even took off Tom Sawyer's hat to reveal himself. "Stop!"

"Ah-ha!" cried the sheriff from the reviewing stand. "It is the traitorous Sir William of Goat! Arrest him!"

The four musketeers pounced forward.

Billy flew back.

Up came the four swirling swords.

Billy took another step back.

"Billy?" wheezed Walter, who was hiding behind him.

"Yeah?"

"This isn't fun anymore."

"Tell me about it."

Billy could feel his heart racing. He had never been so afraid in his life. He and Walter were a long way from the lagoon and the rowboat.

"Some Sunday school picnic this turned out to be," mumbled Walter.

And that gave Billy an idea.

"If you arrest me," he said with all the courage he could muster, "then you have to arrest yourselves."

The sheriff chuckled.

"Arrest ourselves? What foolishness. Musketeers? Haul him away!"

"On a Sunday?" demanded Billy.

"Pardonnez-moi?" said Athos.

"You would dare break the church's number one rule and arrest me on a Sunday?"

"Is today Sunday?" muttered Aramis.

"Uh, hello. This is a *Sunday* school picnic, isn't it?"

"Billy?" whispered Walter. "It's actually Tuesday."

"Not here it isn't," Billy whispered back.

"Oh. Okay. Parallel universe. Gotcha."

The sheriff stomped his feet.

"Curses and foul language! Sir William speaketh most true. Today is indeed Sunday. Therefore, we may not arrest him nor hunt down those other cowardly scoundrels. We cannot do anything until tomorrow!"

The sheriff stepped to the edge of his platform to make a pronouncement.

"Hear ye, hear ye, loyal citizens of Missouri. At noontide tomorrow, Sir William of Goat; that rogue known as Robin Hood; his merry man Hercules; and their newest accomplice, the local scallywag Thomas Sawyer, shall be dragged to the gallows tree, where I shall settle my score with them once and for all. Come, royal deputies!"

Trumpets sounded with a fanfare.

The sheriff and the musketeers marched away.

Well, the musketeers marched. The sheriff limped and said "ouch" a lot.

"That's it?" said Walter in utter disbelief.

"I guess," said Billy.

"We can go home?"

"Yup."

They were both quiet for maybe fifteen seconds.

Then Walter practically erupted with joy. "That was amazing! *You* were amazing! What a story you made up, right on the spot. That bit about this being Sunday? Incredible, Billy. You've got a gift, my friend. A gift."

Billy just laughed. "Come on, Walter. We should leave."

"We're going home, right?"

"Definitely. First we'll find a book to help us save Hercules, Robin Hood, and Tom Sawyer. Afterwards, Tom can help us find the treasure."

"Before we leave," said Walter, "I want to say a quick good-bye to Pollyanna. Maybe try some pie."

"Go ahead. It's Sunday. The sheriff can't bother us anymore. Not today, anyway."

"Incredible!" said Walter. "Absolutely incredible."

Billy agreed. This might turn out to be the most incredible summer of his whole entire life.

That afternoon, Billy and Walter carefully examined the spines of all the books lined up in Dr. Libris's special bookcase, trying to pick the perfect one to resolve all the problems on the island.

"Maybe," said Walter, "you should read *Alice's Adventures in Wonderland* and have her give that bottle of shrinking potion to the Sheriff of Nottingham."

"Not bad," said Billy. "But we might end up with the Queen of Hearts screaming, 'Off with their heads! Off with their heads!' "

"You're right. I'm pretty sure getting your head chopped off is worse than being hanged. Okay, I have another idea."

"What?"

"Well, while you and your mom had lunch, I went home and took a look at *our* copy of *Robin Hood*. I wanted to see if anything we did out on the island changed anything in the story."

"Oh. Good thinking. Did it?"

"Nope. Everything's the same. The Sheriff of Nottingham doesn't limp and he doesn't have four French deputies. The book is fine. It's just the island that's kind of screwy."

"Good."

"So *maybe,*" said Walter, "we don't have to do anything."

"What?"

"Our world is okay. We don't have to worry about theirs."

"Um, yes we do."

"Nuh-unh. We can read new books and have new adventures and find the hidden treasure with somebody besides Tom Sawyer. The people on the island right now really aren't our problem."

"Yes they are. We can't abandon them just because they aren't fun to play with anymore."

"Well," said Walter, "we *could.*"

"But it wouldn't be right, and you know it."

"Yeah. I do." He waited a second. "And when we find the treasure, splitting it fifty-fifty, that'll be the right thing to do, too, correct?"

"Definitely. Unless Tom Sawyer wants to take a cut."

"True. Fair is fair."

* * *

Around six, they finally found the one book they both hoped would scare off the sheriff and stop the musketeers from bickering with everybody else without adding too many new complications: *Journey to the Center of the Earth* by Jules Verne.

Walter went home and Billy settled into the comfy chair to start reading. He didn't hear any sounds but that didn't surprise him.

Most of the action took place underground.

Billy made it all the way to Chapter 40, which was set in a rugged cavern with prickly stalactites dripping down from the ceiling. The subterranean tunnel was filled with "monsters of the deep" and "gigantic fish and animals."

Billy had been reading so long his eyes became heavy.

At two in the morning, he woke up with drool dribbling down his chin.

Half-asleep, Billy put the book away, headed upstairs, crawled into bed, and prayed that some of the prehistoric monsters from the Jules Verne book would stay home at the center of the earth.

No way could they all fit inside Tom Sawyer's cave.

THE THETA PROJECT

LAB NOTE #322

Prepared by

Dr. Xiang Libris, PsyD, DLit

Things are moving along much more rapidly than we anticipated.

Yesterday, the Theta Project produced its first tangible and, therefore, marketable result.

And we have Walter A. to thank.

First he created the character Pollyanna by reading her into being under the dome. Next he brought what had been a by-product of his and Billy G.'s imaginings off the island and into the "real" world.

Walter A. visited Pollyanna's tent at their imaginary Sunday school picnic and procured a slice of huckleberry pie. He then transported this hidden treat off the island, across the lake, and into his cottage, where, we may safely assume, he ate it.

Unfortunately, we do not have cameras inside Walter A.'s home. However, later in the afternoon, while he spent time in my study with Billy G., I did notice a sizeable stain on Walter's shirt.

It was bright red.

From the very real huckleberries in what had once been make-believe pie.

The next morning, Billy slung his backpack over his shoulder and hurried to the Hodgepodge Lodge.

Walter was sitting on the back steps. He was frowning. Alyssa was sitting next to him. She was smiling.

She was also wearing a life jacket.

"Um, what seems to be the problem?" asked Billy.

Walter jerked his thumb at his sister.

"I want to see the island," she whined.

Walter heaved a huge sigh. "I told you, Alyssa. You can't."

"Yes, I can! Mommy said so. She said I could go if I wore a life jacket." She held up her pink backpack. "She even made me a snack."

"Look, Alyssa," Walter pleaded, "not today, okay?"

"Things are a little crazy out there," added Billy. "Tomorrow would be better."

"If you don't take me out to the island *right now,* I'm going to scream so loud Mommy will hear it and so will Mrs. Gillfoyle and so will all the neighbors and then they won't let *anybody* go out to the island ever again!"

Billy looked at Walter.

Walter looked at Billy.

Alyssa smiled proudly.

"Okay," said Billy. "Let's go."

"We're taking her?" said Walter.

"I don't think we have a choice."

When they reached the clearing on the other side of the locked gate, Pollyanna was waiting for them.

"Pollyanna," said Walter, still sort of pouting, "this is my little sister, Alyssa."

"Why, hello, Alyssa," said Pollyanna, dipping into a curtsy. "I'm very glad to make your acquaintance."

"You're pretty," said Alyssa.

"Why, thank you. I think you're pretty, too."

Alyssa held up her backpack. "Would you like some of my snack?"

"My, aren't you precious? Say, do you know what we should do?"

"What?"

"We should have a picnic. Doesn't 'a picnic' sound so much grander than 'a snack'?"

"It does, it does!"

Billy grinned.

This might actually work. Alyssa and Pollyanna could have their picnic in the open field that used to be Paris, Sherwood Forest, and Hercules's wrestling pit. Meanwhile, Billy and Walter would hike to Tom Sawyer's cave, where the prehistoric monster from the Jules Verne book would give everybody from Hercules to D'Artagnan a common enemy—something to fight instead of each other.

It would also scare off the Sheriff of Nottingham for good.

Or so Billy hoped.

"Come on," Billy said to Walter. "Alyssa will be safe here with Pollyanna. Let's go find the others." He pulled Dr. Libris's copy of *Tom Sawyer* out of his backpack and started reading from Chapter 29. " 'The mouth of the cave was up the hillside—an opening shaped like a letter A.' "

"So it has to be up on that mountain that looks like a tooth," said Walter.

Billy nodded. "Its massive oaken door will be unbarred."

"Really?"

"Says so in the book."

"Then let's go! You've got the Jules Verne book, too, right?"

Billy tapped his backpack. "We better hurry. It's nearly noon."

* * *

Billy and Walter followed the narrow path through the forest, crossed the empty Sunday school meadow, and climbed a steep trail into the craggy hills that formed the base of the molar-shaped mountain.

Soon they were edging their way along what was basically a narrow cliff. On one side there was an abrupt one-hundred-foot drop into a leafy abyss; on the other, a sheer wall of gray stone climbing to the sky.

"Look," said Walter. He pointed up the trail to an open wooden door shaped like the letter "A" cut into the face of the mountain.

"That's the entrance to the cave," said Billy.

Behind them, they heard the clomping of heavy boots.

"Quick," said Billy. "We need to hide!"

"Where?"

"In the cave!"

Billy and Walter scampered along the ridge, their feet sending loose pebbles cascading over the edge to patter on the treetops far below.

Fortunately, the trail widened in front of the cave.

The two boys ducked through the doorway. In the deep gloom, Billy could hear a steady *drip, drip, drip* of water plinking from the cavern's ceiling. The chamber was pitch-black and colder than frozen pizza crust. Billy heard Walter do a double pump on his asthma inhaler. He thought he also heard a flap of wings.

Is it a bat? Or one of Jules Verne's hideous make-believe monsters?

Finally, Billy's eyes adjusted to the darkness.

The cave was just like Mark Twain had written it: "a vast labyrinth of crooked aisles that ran into each other and out again and led nowhere."

Looking around, Billy didn't see anybody else. No Tom Sawyer, no Hercules, no Robin Hood, no Maid Marian.

"Where are they?" squeaked a panicked Walter. "They said they'd be hiding here."

Billy put a finger to his lips and led Walter behind a limestone ledge into a cramped side chamber where they could still keep an eye on the mouth of the cave.

Five seconds later, the Sheriff of Nottingham and the four musketeers were standing right outside.

Billy could see their dusty boots.

33

“Huzzah!” cried the sheriff outside the open door. “This is the cave!”

Limping forward, he slid his silver dagger out of its jeweled scabbard.

So much for Tom Sawyer’s cave being such a great hiding place, thought Billy.

D’Artagnan drew his sword and stepped into the dank main chamber.

“Make haste, musketeers!” cried the sheriff. “Illuminate thy lanterns.”

Swinging their sputtering lights, the sheriff and the four swordsmen inched their way deeper into the cavern’s first room. Billy and Walter ducked down behind a short wall of slick stone.

“Billy?” whispered Walter. “Where’s Jules Verne’s underground monster?”

"I dunno."

"We need the monster for the plan to work."

"I know."

"Well, maybe you need to read that bit again."

"Yeah."

Lying down on the cold cave floor, Billy eased the book out of his backpack.

In the flickering lantern light bouncing off the walls above him, he silently reread the scariest paragraphs of Chapter 40.

Nothing happened.

"Maybe you have to read it out loud," suggested Walter. "Like I did with the Junior Wizard card."

"*Voilà!*" cried Athos, holding down his hat plume so it wouldn't scrape against the cave's ceiling. "Are these not footprints?"

Walter nudged Billy with his knee. "Read it, Billy. Read it out loud!"

Billy read as speedily and loudly as he could.

" 'I became aware of something moving in the distance . . .' "

"Ah-ha!" cried the sheriff, waving his lantern back and forth, trying to find Billy in the dark. "Sir William of Goat! I do recognize thy voice!"

Billy, still flat on his back behind the short limestone divider, kept reading. " 'I looked with glaring eyes. One glance told me that it was something monstrous. It was the great "shark-crocodile." . . .' "

"Pardonnez-moi?" said Athos to nobody in particular. "What is this 'shark-crocodile'?"

" 'About the size of an ordinary whale,' " read Billy in reply, " 'with hideous jaws and two gigantic eyes, it advanced. Its eyes fixed on me with terrible—' "

"Run for thy lives!" Robin Hood's and Maid Marian's voices rang out from deep within the cave.

"Oh my!" screamed Tom Sawyer from further down in the maze of tunnels. "Run away!"

The three of them raced up from the darkness, past Billy and Walter's hiding spot, through the entry hall, and out to the sunlit ledge, to which the musketeers had retreated to, once again, strike their "en garde" pose.

"Seize them!" shouted the sheriff.

An earsplitting, rock-shaking, earthquaking roar echoed off the walls of the cavern.

Hercules, still deep inside the cave, shouted, "By Zeus! It is the sharkodile! The most monstrous beast I have ever encountered!"

The musketeers backed away from the mouth of the cave. So did the sheriff, Robin Hood, Maid Marian, and Tom Sawyer.

This is it, thought Billy. *I'm going to be killed by a book.*

He wanted to flee but his legs wouldn't cooperate. His brain said, "Run!" but his bones didn't budge. He was frozen, right where the sharkodile could sniff him out and gulp him down for a quick between-meals snack. Walter was lying right beside him, trying his best to disappear into the stone-slab cave floor.

"Fear not, good friends!" Hercules charged up from the darkness. "The sharkodile shall not harm you this day!"

The muscleman scooped Billy and Walter up off the floor and, cradling them under his gigantic arms like a pair of footballs, hauled them out of the cave to safety.

Or so they hoped.

But it wasn't exactly safe outside the cave.

"Arrest those outlaws!" roared the Sheriff of Nottingham, who was waiting on the cliff. Billy's plan to scare him off with Jules Verne's monster hadn't really worked. "Slap them all in chains!" he yelled.

Nobody listened to him.

Because a hideous creature the size of a school bus—with the scaly green body of a crocodile but the head of a great white shark—thrust its jaws out of the cave and growled. Its breath smelled like moldy cheeseburgers.

"Stand back!" cried Hercules. "For I have battled beasts such as this before."

"Aye!" shouted the sheriff, retreating in fear. "I shalt stand back—all the way back to London!"

"Coward!" cried Maid Marian.

"He who lives and runs away," said the sheriff as he hobbled down the hill, "may live to fight another day!"

Billy ignored the sheriff (who had finally done what Billy knew he would) and focused on the mouth of the cave.

Squirming and squealing, the mammoth sharkodile had wiggled halfway out of the A-shaped entrance.

D'Artagnan lunged at it with his sword.

The beast snapped the steel blade in half as easily as if it were a Twizzler.

Inch by inch, the growling sharkodile squeezed its massive body further and further out of the cave's tight doorway.

"Watch out!" shouted Tom Sawyer. "That thing's gonna pop!"

The sharkodile roared and, with one last gigantic grunt, muscled its way free.

"*Quelle horreur!*" screamed the musketeers as the beast rumbled forward.

The sharkodile took aim at D'Artagnan, the man who had poked at it with his sword. Snarling, it stretched its jaws open as wide as it could. Its teeth were glistening triangles the size of shovel blades.

But an instant before the sharkodile could crush D'Artagnan in its bear-trap jaws, Hercules shoved the young musketeer aside and hurled himself into the giant creature's fearsome mouth.

Feet firmly planted between two razor-sharp incisors, Hercules pressed his hands against the ribbed roof of the monster's humongous mouth to become a human wedge locking the beast's chompers wide open. His arm muscles quivered. His tree-trunk legs shivered. Billy had never seen such a feat of pure bravery and strength. *No wonder they made up myths about the guy,* he thought.

"Robin?" Hercules grunted.

"Aye?"

"Can you hit this darkened tooth? The one closest to my left hand?"

"Aye, marry."

Robin Hood let loose an arrow. It zipped through the air and struck a tooth that was as black as coal. The instant the arrowhead hit, the tooth popped out of the sharkodile's mouth like a flicked kernel of dried corn.

The beast stopped snarling.

Hercules hopped out of the monster's mouth.

Billy couldn't believe his eyes.

The sharkodile actually seemed to smile. Then it started licking Hercules with its very long, extremely wet and sloppy tongue.

"It had a cavity," said Hercules with a titter, because the sharkodile's tongue was tickling. "Needed its tooth pulled. Is that not right, my friend?"

The sharkodile purred.

Feeling better than it probably had in eons, the sharkodile skittered back into the cave and scurried away.

"Yes!" said Billy and Walter triumphantly.

They slapped each other high fives and did a quick little end-zone dance.

"Huzzah!" shouted Hercules, Maid Marian, and Robin Hood.

Athos strode forth and extended his hand.

"Monsieur Hercules, we musketeers are in your debt. You have saved our newest brother, D'Artagnan. Therefore, you and your friends will forever be our brothers, too!"

"No more fighting?" said Hercules.

"*Oui.* Never again shall these four swords be raised against any of you."

"Good friends," proclaimed Robin, "let us abide in peace."

"Indeed," said D'Artagnan. "All for one . . ."

Now everybody shouted: "And one for all!"

Billy felt fantastic. His plan had, after a few false starts, actually worked. Not exactly the way he'd thought it would, but still.

"Don't forget the treasure," whispered Walter.

"Right."

The two boys hurried over to Tom Sawyer. "Tom?" said Billy. "We were wondering. Are you busy later?"

He showed Tom Sawyer the slip of paper from the green bottle.

On this island, you shall find great treasure.

Tom grinned. "I knew it. I told them other boys there'd been pirates on this island before."

"Do you know where they hid their treasure?" asked Walter.

"Oh, it's hid in mighty particular places—sometimes in rotten chests under the end of a limb of an old dead tree, but mostly under the floor in haunted houses."

"Is there a haunted house on this island?" asked Billy.

"I reckon there might could be."

"Billy just has to read about one first," said Walter.

"Huh?" said Tom.

"Never mind," said Billy. "We'll be back. Tomorrow."

"Bring your shovels, boys. And grab a wheelbarrow, too. I wager we'll find so much gold and silver and diamonds, you two can have pie and a glass of soda every day and go to every circus that comes to town."

Billy couldn't believe his good luck.

His mom and dad's money problems were officially over.

All Billy had to do was find a book with a spooky old house in it.

Billy and Walter practically danced back to the clearing to pick up Alyssa, whose picnic with Pollyanna had turned into a tea party. The girls hugged good-bye with promises to do it again. Soon.

The whole boat ride back, they recalled the day's amazing adventures.

"That was so much fun!" said Alyssa.

"But you can't tell Mom or Dad," Walter said to his sister.

Alyssa gave him a look. "Well, *duh*. Every kid knows that."

Billy and Walter were still stoked when they docked the rowboat behind Dr. Libris's cabin.

Until they saw Nick Farkas.

He was climbing onto his Jet Ski with a rolled-up booklet stuffed into his back pocket.

"What's going on out there on the island, bird nerds?" Farkas shouted.

"Nothing," said Billy. "Just, you know, birds."

Alyssa took in a deep breath. "And—"

Walter cupped his hand over her mouth to muffle her.

"If there's nothing going on out there," cried Farkas, "how come you two doofuses keep going back?"

Billy shrugged. "We like birds."

"Is that so? Well, I do, too."

Farkas gunned his Jet Ski and, fumes spewing, blasted off across the water toward the island.

"Billy?" said Walter.

"Yeah?"

"Did you remember to lock the gate?"

"Yeah."

"Good. Because the last thing we want is Nick Farkas finding our treasure before we do."

Billy was still feeling pretty great the next morning.

He already had some good ideas about books with haunted houses in them. Maybe *The Haunting of Hill House* by Shirley Jackson or anything by Edgar Allan Poe.

His mother, on the other hand, didn't look like she felt so good.

They were having breakfast on the back porch. Pancakes, sausage, melted butter, real maple syrup. It should've been fun.

It wasn't.

Instead, it was quiet.

The only sound was the dull scrape of plastic forks on paper plates as Billy and his mother pushed pancake wedges around in syrupy circles.

"So," said Billy. "Walter and I had a blast out on the island yesterday."

His mom looked up from her plate. Forced a smile.

"Great. What do you guys do out there all day?"

"Just goof off. Make up stories."

"You're good at that."

"Goofing off? Mom, I'm the best."

"I meant making up stories. You have a wonderful imagination."

"Thanks. I guess I get it from Dad."

And the frown was back.

"Why don't you ask him about that when he comes up this afternoon?"

"What?"

"Your father called. There's something he wants to talk to us about. Something 'extremely important.' "

"He just dropped me off like four days ago."

"I know."

"Guess he missed us, huh?"

His mom didn't answer.

"I need you here," she said. "When he comes."

"No problem. We'll postpone the treasure hunt."

"Huh?"

"Nothing."

Billy decided not to tell his mother about the message in the bottle until *after* he and Walter struck it rich.

"Finished with your breakfast?"

"Sure. I guess." Billy handed her his plate. He'd only eaten half of one pancake but he'd lost his appetite for any more.

Something was up.

Something bad.

"Your father will probably get here around three."

"Okay," said Billy.

"If I need you sooner, I'll blow the boat horn."

"The what?"

"I found it in a kitchen cabinet. The label claims you can hear its blast a mile away."

"Awesome," said Billy, putting on a big smile—which his mother didn't return. She just carried the wilting paper plates into the kitchen.

As soon as the screen door squeaked shut, Walter and Alyssa padded into the backyard.

Walter looked even more worried than Billy's mom.

He was carrying a thin library book.

"Uh, Billy? We have a problem. A *giant* problem."

THE THETA PROJECT

LAB NOTE #323

Prepared by

Dr. Xiang Libris, PsyD, DLit

Friends and colleagues: we continue to make incredible progress.

In fact, so much is happening so quickly, I feel compelled to relocate from my remote observation post to my secure lab on the island.

Now, more than ever, I feel confident that our research will soon make us all very, very rich!

"I shouldn't even go out to the island today," Billy said to Walter as they tossed their life jackets into the rowboat. "My dad is coming to visit this afternoon. My mom is totally bummed."

"Well, I'm sorry," said Walter. "But hello? The giant from *Jack and the Beanstalk* could be over there. Lives are at stake."

Billy shook his head. "Why'd you let your sister bring a book like that out to the island?"

"I didn't know she had it. It was in her backpack."

"You should've inspected her bag. Like they do at airports."

"Alyssa didn't do this, okay? This is Pollyanna's fault! She's the one who read the book out loud."

"Hey, lame-o's!" Nick Farkas was on his dock chugging

a two-liter bottle of soda. "You heading back to library camp?"

"What?" said Billy.

"On the island. I checked it out yesterday. Met some goofy dork dressed up like Jack from *Jack and the Beanstalk*. Seriously infantile. Just your speed, Waldo. You too, Weedpole."

Great.

Farkas had seen Jack.

Billy worked the oars.

Walter jammed his asthma inhaler into his mouth. Forgot to pump it.

"You can't blame Pollyanna," Billy continued when they were halfway across the lake. "She's not really real."

"Okay. Fine. Pollyanna's not real. But you are, Billy Gillfoyle. And you're the one who opened up this black hole pathway into a parallel universe."

"For the last time, whatever it is, it is *not* a black hole. Those only exist in the vast vacuum of space. We are *not* in the vast vacuum of space."

"Well, we might as well be!" squeaked Walter.

"I agree."

"Good."

"Pump your inhaler."

"Thank you."

"You're welcome."

* * *

Billy and Walter reached the island, still annoyed with each other.

They hiked silently up the path, unlocked the gate, stepped into the clearing, and found themselves standing in an elongated ditch filled with X-shaped mounds lined up in tidy diagonal rows.

The trench had to be seven and a half feet long, maybe three feet wide, and two feet deep.

"What the . . . ," said Billy, staring at the ground and doing some quick mental math.

Walter started wheezing again.

"Uh-oh," said Billy.

He'd just figured out that he and Walter were standing in a humongous boot print. The kind you'd leave behind if you were, oh, fifty feet tall.

Billy shook his head. "Jack's giant is *huge*."

"Oh, goody! I'm so glad you boys came back." Pollyanna waltzed out from the underbrush. "Did you bring Alyssa?"

"Sorry," said Walter, still staring down at the footprint that was ten times bigger than Bigfoot's. "Not today."

"Are you okay?" Billy asked Pollyanna. "Did you see the giant?"

"Oh, yes. He's so surprisingly different. I love creatures who are surprisingly different, don't you?"

"Not really," said Walter. "Not when they're giants."

"So where's everybody else?" asked Billy.

"Off on their next adventures, I suppose. Except, of course, the Sheriff of Nottingham. He's still here."

"No," said Billy, "the sheriff ran away."

"He said he was going to London," added Walter.

"Golly," said Pollyanna. "I guess he was telling you boys a big, fat fib."

Billy remembered the sheriff's parting words: "He who lives and runs away may live to fight another day!"

His mouth felt extremely dry. "So, uh, where's the sheriff?" he asked Pollyanna.

"Well, earlier, I saw him slinking around on his stallion. He was nailing new 'wanted' posters on every tree he could find." Pollyanna pulled a poster out of her wicker basket. "It's ever so much longer than the first one."

WANTED
DEAD OR ALIVE

(PREFERABLY DEAD)

ROBIN HOOD

HIS MERRY PERSON HERCULES

MAID MARIAN

MR. THOMAS SAWYER

AND, MOST URGENTLY,

SIR WILLIAM OF GOAT,

HE WHO DIDST CAUSE ME
TO BE CRIPPLED

—THE SHERIFF OF NOTTINGHAM

38

"Oh, woe is me!"

A young boy in tattered red shorts and a torn red vest slogged out of the forest, a crumpled red elf hat in his hands.

"I think that's Jack," said Walter. "I recognize him from the pictures in Alyssa's library book."

"He looks ever so sad," said Pollyanna. "We should play the glad game with him!"

"First things first," said Billy. "Um, Jack?" He waved at the boy. "Got a second?"

The boy seemed startled.

"Who are you?" he asked. "Do you live in the village?"

"No. But, Jack, we need to stop your giant from squishing everything and everybody on this island. You need to chop down your beanstalk."

"I do? Oh, fiddlesticks!"

"Sorry," said Walter. "It's in the book. I've read it to Alyssa a hundred times."

"So, where's your beanstalk?" asked Billy.

"Why, it grows in the garden—right where my poor widowed mother tossed my magic beans."

"And where exactly is your mother's garden?"

"Right outside our kitchen window."

"Great. Where's the kitchen?"

"Inside our humble hovel of a home."

"Stars and stockings, Jack," said Pollyanna. "Billy needs to know where you live!"

"Come on, you guys," said Walter. "Take it easy on Jack. He's from a book for preschoolers."

"Hear the cow moo," said Jack. "Moo, cow, moo."

"Take us to your house," said Billy very slowly. "We can help you chop down the beanstalk."

"When it 'quivers and shakes from the blows your ax makes,'" said Walter, reciting a memorized verse, "the giant will 'tumble down and break his crown.'"

"Oh, no. I cannot chop down my magic beanstalk. For I have not yet found the goose that lays the golden eggs. My mother and I need at least a dozen golden eggs to live happily ever after."

"And *I* need to be home in a couple hours because my father is coming up to the cabin for a surprise visit and my mother won't eat her pancakes."

Jack blinked a lot. "Pardon?"

"Never mind. It's complicated. But there's not going

to be any 'ever after,' happily or otherwise, if we don't stop your giant from crushing everybody on this island—including you!"

Billy and Walter followed Jack up a winding trail that led them deep into the forest.

Pollyanna didn't go with them. She had to take a jar of jelly to somebody named Mrs. Snow. Apparently, Mrs. Snow lived in a *parallel* parallel universe. Billy figured once you started adding impossibly sideways staircases to your world, you could do it all the way to infinity.

"I spy my house!" cried Jack when they reached a tiny whitewashed cottage near a sunlit field filled with haystacks. A thick green beanstalk, its trunk the size of an oak tree's, grew in the backyard.

"Great," said Billy. "Go grab an ax and we'll—"

Suddenly, the earth started to tremble. Billy nearly toppled over.

"Fee, fi, fo, fum . . ."

Billy looked up. He had to crane his neck way, way back to take in the enormity of what he was facing.

Jack's giant was over fifty feet tall. His head, which was kind of small for his body, cleared the tops of the tallest trees and nearly scraped against the wire mesh dome. He had a bowl-cut hairdo and breathed through his mouth so heavily drool dribbled off his rubbery lips to puddle on the ground below. His belly jiggled with every step he took. So did most of Jack's farm.

Billy, Walter, and Jack ducked behind a haystack.

The giant bent down and plucked the thatched roof right off the top of Jack's tiny cottage.

"Where are you, little thief?" droned the giant. "I can smell you."

He took two enormous sniffs, his swollen nose working like a blubbery bellows to suck up straw and dust with each huff.

"Oh, dear," whispered Jack.

"What?" said Walter.

"Yesterday, my mother was sacking black pepper for the miller man and—"

"A-a-a-choo!"

The giant was seized by an enormous sneeze.

The hot blast hit the haystack like a typhoon and sent straw flying. The three boys were blown backward in a snotty wind tunnel, right out into the open.

Right where the giant could see them.

Enormous knees creaking, he rose to his full height.

"You!" The giant pointed at Jack with a finger the size of a pool noodle. "You are the little thief who stole my singing harp!"

The giant took one giant step forward.

"Run!" shouted Billy.

He took off with Jack and Walter close behind. They

dashed between the giant's booted feet and raced toward a tight tangle of twisting trails.

"Whaaa?" The giant bent at the waist, tucked his head between his legs, and watched the fleeing boys. "Why are you children upside down?"

After maybe ten minutes in a maze of trees Billy and Walter had not yet explored, they came to a tall chain-link fence. A squat cinder-block building with dark tinted windows sat in a small clearing on the other side. A satellite dish was mounted on its roof.

"What's that?" said Walter.

"I don't know," said Billy. "But we should hide in there!"

Walter jiggled the gate. "It's locked."

"I'll climb over it," said Jack. "I'm good at climbing."

He grabbed hold of the fencing.

ZZZZT!

It sparked and crackled. The jolt nearly knocked Jack out of his pointy-toed boots.

"It's electrified!" said Billy.

"So it'd be perfect to hide behind," said Walter. He rattled the gate again. The gate wasn't electrified, but it was still locked.

"Never fear," said Jack. "I'll be nimble, I'll be quick!"

"Um, I think that's the wrong story," said Walter.

"Never mind," said Billy. "We can use it. Go!"

Jack scurried up a nearby tree to a branch that stretched out over the electrified fence. In no time he was safe on the ground on the other side—which was a good thing.

Because the earth started quaking again.

"Fee, fi, fo, fum!"

The giant thrashed through the forest.

He was close, and coming closer.

39

"Hide behind that building!" Billy shouted at Jack. "Hurry."

Jack ran behind the cinder-block structure.

"N-n-now what?" said Walter as the whole forest trembled every time the giant stepped closer.

"We need to make up our own fairy tale," said Billy.

The giant shoved aside two leafy treetops and peered down at Billy and Walter.

"Fee, fi, fo, fum! I smell the blood of an Englishman!"

Walter wheezed and pumped. Wheezed and pumped.

"Jack's not here," said Billy as coolly as he could.

"Where did he go?"

"Upstairs." He jabbed his thumb toward the sky.

"That little thief stole my magic harp."

"We know. He told us. And while you're wasting your time down here, chasing after Walter and me, Jack's back up in the clouds grabbing your goose, the one that lays the golden eggs."

"No!" said the giant, turning his massive body around as quickly as he could, which wasn't very quickly at all. "He cannot have Goldie!"

"Then you better hurry home to protect her."

"I will!"

And off he lumbered. Slowly. Very, very slowly. Each step thudded like it was taken by a twenty-ton elephant wearing cement work boots.

When the giant was finally out of sight, Walter was able to breathe a little easier.

"So, he's going to climb back up the beanstalk to his castle in the sky?"

"Yup," said Billy. "We'll give him a five-minute head start. Then we'll run back to Jack's house, find an ax, and—"

A sharp reflection of something silver flared through the trees.

Billy grabbed Walter and pulled him down behind the nearest clump of shrubs.

A gangly six-foot-tall gecko—dressed in a shiny silver space suit—crept through the forest toting a silver ray gun. His curled silver tail slithered along the forest floor behind him.

"I don't believe this," said Billy.

"W-w-what?" stammered Walter. "Wh-wh-who is that?"

"The Space Lizard."

The crazy island was spinning wildly out of control.

"Who?" asked Walter in a panicky whisper.

"From the comic books and video games."

The Space Lizard flicked out his tongue and nabbed a robin's egg from a nearby nest.

When the mother bird squawked, the Space Lizard hissed at her. His acidic spit shriveled a clump of leaves and blackened the branches of the tree.

"He eats eggs?" asked Walter.

"He collects them," Billy explained. "Different eggs are worth different points."

The Space Lizard had his visor rolled up into his astronaut helmet, exposing his long, twitchy snout, beady black eyes, and flittering tongue. His acid-blaster ray gun had so many bulges and bubbles along its barrel it looked like it had been designed by a guy who also made balloon poodles.

In the distance, Billy could see the giant climbing up the beanstalk, which had poked a hole in the mesh dome. He was telephone-poling his way toward a towering cauliflower of a cloud, which, when the sunlight shifted, really did look like a cotton-candy castle in the sky.

"Fee, fi, fo, fum!" The giant's voice boomed like rolling thunder through the air. "I've come to get you, Englishman!"

The Space Lizard heard the giant, too. He twitched his head sideways. Tilted it up. Twitched it some more.

And then the Space Lizard hopped over a stump and

darted into the thick forest. It looked like he might be heading to Jack's house.

Billy and Walter stood up.

"Billy? How did a monster from a video game end up on our island?"

"I don't know. Maybe when Nick Farkas came out here yesterday, he brought along a couple of his *Space Lizard* comic books or that cheat guide his mother bought him."

An ear-piercing boat horn blared in the distance.

"That's my mom," said Billy. "I've gotta go. My dad's here."

"But the giant," said Walter. "When he finds out you were just making that stuff up about Jack and the goose, he'll climb back down."

"It'll be okay. Jack's safe."

"Yes, I am!" shouted Jack from behind the cinder-block building.

Walter was still worried. "But what about the treasure? How can we dig it up if the Space Lizard—"

"Walter, my dad is here. My mom needs me. We'll come back later to deal with everything else."

"B-b-but—"

"Later!"

40

"Good luck at home," said Walter once the rowboat was tied up at the dock.

"Thanks."

"If you need anything . . ."

"I'll let you know."

Walter took off for the Hodgepodge Lodge. Billy made his way toward Dr. Libris's cabin.

He noticed cookout supplies spread across the backyard. A small charcoal grill. Fancy barbecue cooking utensils that all matched. A grocery sack filled with marshmallows, chocolate bars, and graham crackers.

His dad probably brought all that junk up from the city. He loved making s'mores, even in their apartment's toaster oven.

Billy picked up his pace.

His mom and dad were nowhere in sight.

So he headed around the side of the cabin and into the driveway, where he saw his dad's convertible. A bunch of grocery bags were lined up on the gravel behind the rear bumper.

And then he heard his parents.

It sounded like they were around the corner, talking on the front porch.

"You really want to do a cookout, Bill?" he heard his mother say.

"It's what we always do at the lake," said his dad.

"That was a long time ago."

"I thought it might make this . . . easier."

"For who?"

"For Billy. Where is he, anyway?"

"In a hurry to tell him your big news?"

Billy held on to the side of his dad's car for support.

He didn't know what to do.

So he put on a brave smile and rounded the corner. It was time to play the real, live glad game.

"Hey, Dad!"

"There you are!" Billy's father came down the porch steps and gave Billy a bear hug. "How you doin', kiddo?"

"Not bad. How's New York?"

"Crazy busy. Oh, that reminds me." His dad broke out of the hug and went back to the porch to retrieve the shoulder bag he carried to work instead of a briefcase. "I swung by the Apple Store."

He handed Billy a brand-new iPhone.

"Your mom told me what happened to your old one. Ouch."

"That's an early birthday gift, Billy," said his mother.

"That's right," said his dad. "Your mom and I talked about it. We both agreed."

Billy took the iPhone. His birthday wasn't till September. Did this mean his mom and dad weren't getting back together after the summer?

His dad had the queasy look on his face that he always got right before he had to say something grown-up-ish instead of silly.

"Well, I better, um, go inside and charge it," said Billy.

"Your dad wants to talk to you," said his mom, sounding even sadder than she had at breakfast. Guess this story wasn't turning out the way she wanted it to, either.

"Yeah," said his father. "We need to talk."

"Okay. But right now I want to, you know . . ." He waggled the iPhone.

"Sure," said his dad. "We'll talk later. We're putting together a little cookout."

"I saw. I'll be upstairs in my room."

Billy went into the cabin, ran up the steps, and flopped down face-first onto his bed. He didn't even plug in his shiny new iPhone.

He just wished he could head back to the island, where, sooner or later, stories seemed to find their happy endings.

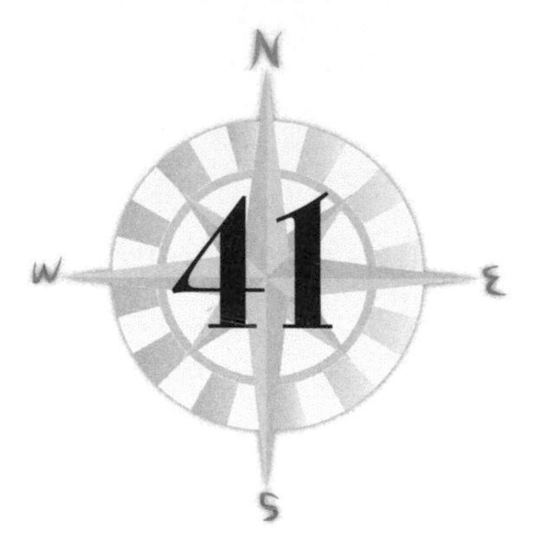

Billy spent the rest of the afternoon avoiding his parents.

He figured if they couldn't sit him down for "the talk," they couldn't tell him their news. From the look on his mother's face, he could guess it wasn't anything good.

He decided he'd try to sneak downstairs. Hide over at Walter's place.

But his dad caught him at the back door.

"Hey, Billy," his dad said, gesturing toward two lawn chairs. "Got a minute?"

"Well, I really wanted to run next door. Show my friend Walter my new iPhone."

"Okay," said his mom, coming down from the cabin with a small cooler filled with drinks. "But dinner is at six."

"Can Walter come?"

"Not tonight, hon. Family only. Okay?"

Billy nodded.

And he ran over to Walter's house.

Walter's bedroom was under the upside-down boat section of the Hodgepodge Lodge.

Billy plugged his new iPhone into the wall so he and Walter could load it up with apps.

"This house is so awesome," said Billy.

"Yeah," said Walter. "Dr. Libris liked it, too. He'd always say my dad had an amazing imagination. Then he'd say something like 'too bad you're not Walter's age,' and they'd both laugh."

"Why?"

Walter shrugged. "They're grown-ups. Who knows why grown-ups laugh at anything?"

His mom came into the boat bedroom with a plate of homemade cookies.

"Thanks for taking Alyssa out to the island," she said. "That was sweet of you boys."

"You're welcome," said Billy.

The instant Mrs. Andrews was gone, Walter took in a deep breath. "You know, Billy, I've been thinking. And you were right. It *was* my fault. I shouldn't've let Alyssa go out to the island with *Jack and the Beanstalk*."

"Don't worry. We'll take care of it."

"When?"

"Tomorrow. I promise."

Walter sniffed the air. "Are you guys grilling burgers?"

"Yeah. And hot dogs."

"Can I come over?"

"Sorry. I asked. They said it's family-only tonight."

"Seriously?"

"Seriously."

"This sounds bad, Billy. Way bad."

"Yeah. Tell me about it."

"You want another burger?" Billy's dad asked.

"Sure," said Billy.

"That's your third one!"

Billy was still stalling. He burped to make enough room for his next burger.

"Billy?" his mom whispered when his dad was back at the grill. "I know this is hard, but you really need to talk with your father."

"I don't want to."

"But you need to." She took a breath and looked Billy square in the eyes. "He's going to L.A."

"To film more commercials?"

"No. He sold one of his screenplays."

Billy brightened. He and Walter might not need to find that treasure after all. "That means he'll make a ton of money, right?"

"Yes," she answered carefully. "It also means he wants to live out there. Permanently."

Billy refused to meet her gaze. "Cool," he said casually. "I could learn how to surf."

"Billy? You and I will be staying here. Well, not *here*. We'd keep the apartment in the city while your dad . . ."

Billy wanted to jab his fingers in his ears and scream, "NAH, NAH, NAH, NAH!" so he wouldn't have to hear any more of this. Instead, he blurted, "How about marshmallows?"

"Billy? Did you hear what I just said?"

"One burger, coming up!" his dad called from the grill.

"I changed my mind," Billy called back, standing up from the picnic table. "I'm ready for dessert. I'm going to gather up some green sticks so we can toast those marshmallows."

Billy rushed over to the stand of trees bordering Walter's backyard.

"Hi, Billy."

It was Alyssa.

"What're you guys doing?"

Billy wasn't sure what to tell her, exactly. "Uh, getting ready to toast some marshmallows."

"How come you're not camping with Walter?"

"What?"

"Walter told Mom that you guys were spending the night out on the island. He packed up his sleeping bag and everything."

Billy looked toward the island.

What was Walter trying to do?

"When did he leave?"

"About an hour ago. Right after you went home. He took our canoe."

Billy's mind raced.

Walter could get in serious trouble all by himself on the island.

Especially at night.

Especially if the giant climbed back down the beanstalk—not to mention that an alien lizard from an extremely violent video game was hopping around spritzing everything it could find with hydrochloric acid.

"Billy?"

"What?"

"Tell Walter to bring back my library book."

"Huh?"

"*Jack and the Beanstalk.* He took that out to the island, too."

42

Billy snatched a couple of twigs off the ground.

He had to get back to the island, fast.

It was time to wrap up the family cookout, even if that meant sitting down and talking with his dad.

"You know what?" he said. "I'm stuffed. Here's some sticks. You guys can toast marshmallows without me. What do you want to talk about, Dad?"

His mom dropped her head and walked away.

His dad got that queasy face again. He scooted two lawn chairs around on the grass so they were facing each other. Billy sat down. His father took a seat and put on his serious grown-up face.

"Son, as you may have noticed, your mom and I . . ."

"BLAH, BLAH, BLAH, BLAH, BLAH," was all Billy heard for the next five, maybe ten, minutes.

Finally, his father finished. "We just think it'll be best for everybody."

"So when are you leaving?" Billy asked. "Right now?"

"No. I'm going to spend the night. Sleep in the living room."

Billy just nodded.

"Well, I'm glad we could have this talk."

Grown-ups always said that.

Apparently, talking made them feel better, even when the same talk made a kid feel worse.

"Can I be excused now?" Billy asked, the way he would if they were at the dinner table back home.

"Oh. Sure. Guess you need some time to think about all this, huh?"

"Yeah."

The sun was starting to set.

Night was falling.

Walter was all alone on the island.

Well, actually, he *wasn't* alone.

And that was the problem.

43

Billy hurried down to the dock.

"Where are you going, hon?" his mom called from the back porch.

"Out to the island."

"It's getting dark."

"I'll be okay. My new iPhone has a flashlight app."

"Okay. Be sure to wear—"

Billy held up his life jacket before she could say it.

His mom hugged herself like she was cold, and headed back into the cabin.

Billy docked at the island just as the sun set.

When he reached the field on the far side of the gate, he saw Robin Hood, Maid Marian, Hercules, Tom Sawyer, and Pollyanna. All of them were sitting on logs set up in a semicircle, and they were staring at something on the ground.

Billy flicked on his flashlight app and waved his iPhone.

"You guys? It's me. Have any of you seen Walter?"

"Yes," said Hercules. "As soon as Pollyanna told us that Walter was alone on the island, we came rushing back."

"And," said Robin, "we were most surprised to learn that thou, Sir William, were not here assisting valiant Walter in his noble quest."

"Robin?" said Maid Marian, shaking her head. "Leave Billy be."

"I'm sorry," mumbled Billy. "I had this thing. With my parents. So, where is he?"

"In trouble," said Hercules.

"Why? What'd he do?"

"He read a book," said Tom Sawyer. "All about that beanstalk fellow, Jack."

"It was a good story," said Hercules. "Action. Adventure. Glory."

"I was glad to hear it," added Pollyanna.

"And, verily," said Robin Hood, "Walter did read that story straight through to its conclusion, whereupon the giant did tumble from the clouds."

"Walter proved himself to be a most courageous giant slayer," said Maid Marian proudly. "The most courageous I e'er did see."

Billy was relieved. "Walter slayed the giant?"

"Aye," said Maid Marian. "Quite handily."

Billy had to grin. Walter had finally found something he was excellent at: slaying giants.

"Jack and his mother got them that goose what lays the golden eggs," said Tom.

"And," said Maid Marian, "that didst upset the leaping lizard mightily."

Billy swallowed hard. "Was this lizard dressed all in silver?"

"Aye," said Robin.

"By and by," said Tom, "this here silvery lizard fellow comes hopping along, hissing and spitting mad."

"He was upset about the eggs," said Hercules. "Blamed Walter."

"Swore each of those golden orbs to be worth one million points, whatever a 'point' might be," added Robin Hood.

"So then what happened?" Billy asked.

"He captured Walter," said Pollyanna.

"Put him in a pointy-tipped prison on stilts with smoke pouring out of its bottom," added Hercules.

"I reckon it was a rocket ship," said Tom. "I seen one once in a book by that feller Jules Verne."

"We strove to free young Walter from the clutches of the beast," said Maid Marian. "But alas, the demon didst pour forth from its weapon a stream of molten acid so fierce none of us dared cross it."

"There was nothing any of us couldst do," said Robin.

Billy couldn't believe what he was hearing. The Space Lizard had captured Walter.

He had him locked up in the Galaxy Blaster.

Billy looked at the ground and finally realized what everybody had been staring at.

Walter's bright red asthma inhaler.

"Walter won't be able to breathe," said Billy. "Not without his asthma medicine."

"We ought to give him a proper funeral," said Tom. "We could have Pollyanner read us a prayer. A good, generous one."

"I know all sorts of good funeral things to say," Pollyanna replied. "Of course, it's awfully hard to play the glad game when someone dies."

Billy slumped down on a log beside Maid Marian. "I never should've dragged Walter into this mess."

Marian placed a gentle hand on Billy's knee. "Aye, but thou didst. Wilt thou now abandon him to the loathsome lizard?"

Billy shook his head. "No. Of course not."

Billy wasn't going to do to Walter what his father was about to do to Billy.

But how could he defeat the Space Lizard? Even Hercules wasn't strong enough to battle a monster with so many powerful weapons.

"Ho, lads and lassies!" said Robin Hood. "All is not lost! Look you, Sir William—I remember a time when Sir Guy of Gisbourne held me captive in his tower. Did my band of merry followers let a moat or castle walls stand in their way?"

"Nay!" said Marian. "Little John and I didst lead the charge. Oh, how the arrows did fly that day!"

"I'm not Little John," Billy said quietly. "Or you, Maid Marian. I'm not a hero." He looked down at the inhaler. "I'm just a kid who can't even save his own family."

"Nonsense," said Maid Marian. "Each of us can choose who or what we shall be. We write our own stories, Sir William. We write them each and every day."

"And," added Hercules, "if you write it boldly enough, others will write about you, too."

Billy stood up. "Where did the Space Lizard take Walter?"

"To his rocket ship," said Tom. "It's parked in the same spot where we had us that Sunday school picnic."

Billy bent down to scoop up the red asthma inhaler. "He needs this."

"By jingo," said Tom, "we might could fling it to him."

"I'm sure Walter would be glad to have it," added Pollyanna.

"Aye!" said Robin Hood. "We could affix it to an

arrow and send it sailing through the porthole of his pointy-tipped dungeon."

"Um," said Billy. "What if you missed?"

"Miss? Ah-ha-ha-ha!"

Billy crept through the underbrush with Robin Hood, Maid Marian, Hercules, and Tom Sawyer.

Pollyanna had to go home, because her Aunt Polly was "ever so worried" about her.

Soon they were in the meadow. Billy could make out the silhouette of the Space Lizard's Galaxy Blaster—an old-fashioned-looking rocket ship shaped like a football propped on a four-legged stand. Yellow light glowed from the single round window in the center of the craft.

"Looky there," said Tom. "That window's cracked open a mite but there ain't nary a three-inch gap betwixt its rim and the sides of the ship."

"Ha!" laughed Robin. "Three inches is more than I require. Make haste. Prepareth the projectile."

Tom quickly lashed the asthma inhaler to the shaft of Robin Hood's arrow with some twine he kept balled up in the back pocket of his blue jeans.

Robin nocked the arrow. After adjusting his aim, he let go of the string. The arrow sliced through the air and slipped through the slender crack beside the circular window. Billy heard the arrowhead *THUNK* as it hit the metal walls inside the Galaxy Blaster.

"Bull's-eye!" said Tom.

"Huzzah!" cried Robin and Marian.

"Thanks, you guys!" shouted Walter from somewhere inside the spaceship. "I needed that."

"Use it right away, Walter," said Billy.

Walter's face popped up at the porthole. "Billy? Is that you?"

"Yeah. Hey—way to go taking care of Jack and the giant."

"It was actually pretty easy. . . ."

"Are you okay?"

"Well, I was until you guys started shooting arrows and shouting 'huzzah' and stuff. Now the Space Lizard is sort of eyeballing me."

"Has he hurt you?"

"No. He's too busy eating dinner. Freeze-dried scrambled bugs. It's in a toothpaste tube like astronauts eat out of."

"So you're safe?"

"Yeah. But, Billy, can you go back to Dr. Libris's study and find a book to bust me out of here? Maybe something where somebody escapes from a prison?"

"Sssilencccce!" hissed a hideous voice.

Walter stepped away from the round window just as a slimy tongue slithered along its edge, sizzling the rubber seal with bubbling acid.

"Be gone from this placccce. All of you!"

The Space Lizard's voice sounded like sandpaper on shattered glass.

Billy stood his ground.

"Look, Mr. Lizard—if you want another shot at grabbing those golden eggs, you better not hurt my friend Walter."

"Really? Why not?"

Billy needed to make up another story. Fast.

"Because tomorrow, if you don't hurt him, Walter can bring it all back. He just has to read that *Jack and the Beanstalk* book out loud again. If he's dead, he can't do that."

Billy didn't really know if Walter could read the giant back to life. He only knew he needed to buy his friend more time.

"Can't sssomeone elsssse do thisss reading?"

"Nope. Walter's the magic reader. He reads the book, Jack comes back. The beanstalk comes back. The castle in the clouds and the goose and all the golden eggs come back, too."

"Why can't he do thisss for me now?"

"Because, uh, the story starts in the morning. Right, Walter?"

"Yes! It does! It says, 'One morning Milky White'—that's the cow—'Milky White gave no milk.' "

"So Jack takes the cow to the market," said Billy, "*in the morning*. He trades the cow for the magic beans *in the morning*. His mom flings the beans out the window *in the morning*. If you really want your golden eggs, just wait till tomorrow. In the morning!"

There was a long pause.

Finally, the Space Lizard hissed, "I ssshall do as you sssuggessst. But if thisss boy doesss not give me my eggsss firssst thing tomorrow—"

"Don't worry," said Billy. "He will. Walter's very talented."

"Um, Billy?" peeped Walter.

"Yeah?"

"Slight problem."

"What's wrong?"

"Well, I don't know if anybody told you about the acid bath Mr. Lizard spewed all over the place when he kidnapped me, but some of it splashed on the *Jack* book. Burnt a big hole straight through the cover and all the pages."

"So you need another copy?"

"Yeah. Dr. Libris probably has one in his bookcase. *Jack and the Beanstalk* is a classic."

"You best run fetch it," said Tom.

"Do not worry about Walter," said Robin.

"We four shall stand guard here all night," added Hercules. "I'd go into that tin can right now and clobber the beast, but . . ."

"He hath that brutal weapon," said Maid Marian. "Just make certain thou returneth before dawn's first light, Sir William. And"—she lowered her voice—"also make certain thou bringeth us a sound battle plan for defeating yon lizard."

Billy nodded. "You're sure you guys can keep Walter safe tonight?"

"I will lay down my life for him if any hint of true harm should come his way," said Hercules. "It is what we heroes do."

"Flee, Sir William!" cried Robin. "Bring us back the magic book!"

When Billy snuck back into the cabin, he could hear his dad in the living room, snoring on the couch.

He tiptoed into Dr. Libris's study.

He scanned the bookcase and found a slim antique book titled *Jack and the Beanstalk and Other Stories.*

Billy thought about taking the *Jack* book right back out to the island.

But he'd made up that whole story about everything happening "in the morning." If he went to rescue Walter in the middle of the night, the Space Lizard might become suspicious and start spewing acid all over the place again.

Besides, while rowing home across the lake, he had come up with a real "battle plan."

First, tomorrow Walter would conjure up Jack again and send him running off to Tom Sawyer's cave. In search of the eggs, the Space Lizard would chase after Jack.

Hercules, Robin Hood, and Maid Marian would protect Jack until he was safely hidden. Meanwhile, Billy would read up the sharkodile. The two monsters would battle it out on the cliff. The sharkodile would surely win. It would be just like rock, paper, scissors. A sharkodile *had* to beat a Space Lizard. While all that was going on, Billy could rescue Walter.

Billy set an alarm on his iPhone. He'd wake up an hour before sunrise and be back on the island with the two books before dawn.

He made his way up the steps to his bedroom. He knew he should get some sleep, even though he also knew he probably couldn't. Not with Walter imprisoned by a hideous comic book beast from a video game rated "M" for "Mature" because it contained "intense violence, blood, and gore."

"Sorry, Walter," he mumbled aloud.

Then he sat down at the little desk under the open window, where he figured he'd find a better signal for his new iPhone. He needed to kill some time. Maybe download a new game.

Or read a comic book.

One where the Space Lizard lost to the good guys.

Billy fired up his favorite comics reader app and found an issue titled *The Space Lizard Meets His Match.*

How'd they do it? Billy wondered. *How'd they defeat the Space Lizard?*

If the comic had a better idea, Billy would borrow it.

Finally, on the second-to-last page of panels, he found his answer.

The Space Lizard "met his match" when a lizard called the Intergalactic Gecko Girl slithered past his rocket ship. The two of them fell in love, got married, and rocketed off to "boldly destroy" new planets and civilizations together for the rest of their lives.

It was totally lame.

Billy flopped onto his bed and stared at the ceiling.

There was one knot in the pine planks that sort of looked like an angry ogre's face.

Or maybe a witch with bumpy warts.

Then again, it could be Abraham Lincoln.

He must've dozed off, because he woke up with a jolt when something tapped against the outside wall.

Billy ignored it. He needed to sleep. If he was going back to face the Space Lizard in the morning, he needed to be rested and ready to rumble. He tried to fluff up his lumpy pillow.

A couple of seconds later, he heard another *clunk*.

Then a pebble flew through the open window and into the room.

"Whoops, sorry," he heard a familiar voice whisper down in the yard. "I'm still not very good at chucking rocks."

Billy went to the window. "Walter?"

Walter was waving up at him.

"Awesome escape plan, Billy!"

"What?"

"Okay, I'm in the rocket ship. You pretend like you're heading home to grab a fresh copy of *Jack and the Beanstalk* and—*BOOM!* Less than an hour later, the Space Lizard gets this crazy, googly-eyed look on his face. He shouts, 'I love you, Gecko Girl!' Then he shoves open the hatch, leaps down to the ground, and grabs this even uglier lizard's hand. They started making goo-goo eyes at each other, which, by the way, is an extremely gross thing to see lizards do, because their eyeballs are so huge on the sides of their heads. Anyway, while they were doing all that, I ran away."

"You're kidding."

"Nope. You're a genius."

"Hang on," Billy said. "I'm coming down."

He dashed down the stairs and out into the yard, gently shutting the back door so he wouldn't wake his dad.

"My hero!" said Walter, slapping him a high five. "You've still got it, Billy!"

"But I'm telling you, I didn't do anything."

"You didn't read up a girlfriend for the Space Lizard?"

"Not on purpose. I mean, I read a stupid comic book on my iPhone where that kind of happened, but . . ."

"Nice! You're so good you've gone digital! Hey, do you guys have any potato chips or marshmallows left over from your cookout? I'm starving. The Space Lizard didn't serve me any supper. Then I had to sprint through the woods and paddle home. By the way—I'm getting much better at canoeing now."

Billy smiled. "There's some food in the kitchen. I'll grab it. Try to keep quiet out here. My mom is working and my dad is asleep already."

"Seriously? Wow. I'm so pumped I may never sleep again!"

Billy crept back into the cabin and raided the kitchen.

While he gathered up the potato chips, a whole blueberry pie his dad must've bought at the Red Barn, some potato salad, and an almost full bag of marshmallows, he started thinking.

Maybe Walter was right.

Maybe he still had "it"—whatever "it" might be.

Maybe Maid Marian was right, too.

Maybe Billy could write his own story and have it turn out the way he wanted it.

Billy cradled all the food against his chest, except the blueberry pie, which he balanced in his hand.

It was the pie that was giving Billy an idea about how he might be able to save his parents' marriage.

* * *

Walter was waiting for him at the picnic table in the backyard.

"I brought you some chips, potato salad, and marshmallows," Billy said.

"Sweet." Walter dug in.

After he'd wolfed down half a bag of chips, scooped up a gob of potato salad, and stuffed a ball of six wadded-up marshmallows into his mouth, Billy figured it was time for the two of them to go to work.

"You still have your Magical Battical cards, right?"

Walter nodded. His mouth was too full of marshmallow mush for him to speak.

"Good. We're going to need them."

"No problem," said Walter, smacking his lips. "Can I have some of that pie?"

"Not right now. We're going to need it, too."

"Hey, Billy? Do you think the Space Lizard is gone for good?"

Billy shook his head. "No. He'll be back. And he might bring his new girlfriend with him. But first things first. Go grab the cards. We also need H. G. Wells's *The Time Machine*."

Walter laughed. "We're gonna mess with the space-time continuum?"

"Yup. But first we have to head over to Nick Farkas's house."

Walter stopped laughing. "But it's, you know—late. Farkas might punch us or something."

"It's a risk I'm willing to take."

"Really? Why?"

"Because Nick Farkas might be the only kid around here who knows how to totally annihilate the Space Lizard."

“I should punch you in the face, Weedpole. You too, Waldo.”

Nick Farkas stood on the other side of the screen door. He was holding a huge bowl of chocolate chip ice cream smothered with whipped cream.

Over Farkas’s shoulder, Billy saw a freeze-frame of the Space Lizard clutching his throat. His eyes were popping out of the scaly slits on both sides of his head like bloodshot bowling balls.

“I’m right in the middle of slaying the Lizard,” said Farkas. *“Again.”*

“Wow,” said Billy, acting even more impressed than he really was. “You slayed him?”

“It’s easy. Once you figure out how.”

“How?” asked Walter, his voice cracking on the “ow.”

“That’s for me to know and you to find out.”

"He's right," said Billy. "We can't expect Nick to tell us all his secrets just so we can go back to the island and win the prize."

Farkas arched an eyebrow. "What prize?"

"Something absolutely amazing!"

"What do I have to do to win it?"

"Defeat the Space Lizard."

"What?"

"It's part of the library camp. Out on the island."

"No way. That camp's for nerds."

"That's what all the cool kids kept saying, so the library decided to run these late-night holographic video games to coolify their camp."

"You're making this up."

"Nope," said Billy. "Right now, out on that island, the Space Lizard is running around blasting acid at everybody."

"It's fake acid, though, right?"

"I don't know," said Walter. "I saw it sizzle through a library book."

"Seriously?" Farkas was getting excited.

"And wait till you see the Space Lizard," said Billy.

"Who is it? Some geek in an aluminum foil astronaut costume with a Super Soaker squirt gun?"

"No. It's the real deal. An interactive 3-D video-laser projection. Like the computer-generated monsters they make for movies."

Farkas squinted at the island. "And they're doing all this out there right now? At eleven-thirty at night?"

"Well, yeah," said Billy. "It's kind of a campout, too."

"So let's go," said Farkas, opening the screen door and stepping out.

"You *do* know how to defeat the Space Lizard, right?"

"Well, duh. I mean, if they've set up their 3-D version like the video game."

"Oh, it's exactly like the video game," said Billy. Under his breath he added, "Or the comic book."

"Good. I memorized all the cheat codes." Farkas jabbed a thumb over his shoulder. "Should I grab my controller?"

"Nope. You play the game through an app you have to download at the library."

"Oh, man," muttered Farkas.

"Don't worry." Billy tapped his backpack. "I've got it on my iPhone. You tell me what moves to make, and I'll key 'em in."

"Fine. But when I win, we are *not* sharing the prize."

"Of course not," said Billy.

"Obviously," added Walter. "The prize is all yours."

"So what are we waiting for?" said Farkas. "We need to be out on that island!"

"You want to take my rowboat?" offered Billy.

"I have a canoe," said Walter.

"No way. We'll take my Jet Ski. It's faster."

“Here’s the key,” Billy said to Walter as he raised the flap so they could all step under the dome. “I’ll meet you guys at the gate.”

“Hurry,” said Farkas. “I’m ready to kick some serious Space Lizard butt.”

“Uh, right this way,” said Walter, escorting Farkas up the dark trail. “Watch out for that—”

“Ouch.”

“Rock.”

When Walter and Farkas were gone, Billy unzipped his backpack. Inside was the junk he carried around every day plus the blueberry pie from the Red Barn and the copy of H. G. Wells’s *The Time Machine* that he’d grabbed out of Dr. Libris’s bookcase. He hadn’t wanted to read the book in front of Farkas, so he read it now.

"It took two years to make," retorted the Time Traveller. "Now I want you clearly to understand that this lever, being pressed over, sends the machine gliding into the future, and this other reverses the motion. Presently, I am going to press the lever, and off the machine will go. It will vanish . . ."

Billy hoped that paragraph would do the trick.

He stuffed the book back into his pack.

Everything set, he hurried up the trail. Walter and Farkas were standing in the center of the first empty meadow. Near the edge of the field, Billy saw something shimmering in the moonlight that made him smile.

H. G. Wells's time machine.

It looked like a steampunk sleigh made out of curved brass railings and burnished wood, with a leather bench seat in its center and a giant brass clock attached to its back. The ivory-handled "future" and "past" levers were mounted up front on a control drum, also made out of glittering brass and glimmering quartz.

Suddenly, somewhere off in the distance, the Space Lizard hissed.

"Oh, don't be mad because she said your tongue is ugly," Billy heard Pollyanna say. "Just be glad that you have such a marvelous flyswatter."

Now the Space Lizard screeched like a crazed dinosaur. Billy guessed he didn't like playing Pollyanna's glad game.

"Man, the sound effects out here are awesome," said Farkas.

The three boys hurried across the clearing.

"Dudes?" said Farkas. "What's with the sled?"

Billy thought fast. "I think it's an arts and crafts project."

Pollyanna skipped into the meadow.

Her plaid dress was covered with sticky burrs. Her straw hat was lopsided on top of her head. Her freckled cheeks were flushed, and the flowers in the dainty basket draped over her arm were scorched black.

But she was still smiling.

And Farkas was smiling, too. In fact, he was beaming.

"Uh, h-h-hello," he stammered. "Are you, um, a librarian?"

"Oh, heavens no. Though I wish I were. Librarians are ever so kind. I wonder, young man, if I might prevail upon *your* kindness this evening?"

"Please," said Farkas, smoothing down his spiky hair. "Prevail away."

"Why, thank you. It seems I made a rather unfortunate enemy this evening after I gave his girlfriend a whole huckleberry pie." She giggled. "One taste and the Gecko Girl flew straight home to share my pie with her mother. Anyway, this other reptile—"

The insanely angry Space Lizard leapt out of the darkness.

Farkas jumped between Pollyanna and the monster.

"Gillfoyle?" he barked. "Type 'P.B.C.'!"

"What?"

"P.B.C.! It's a cheat code."

Billy opened the Notes app on his phone and tapped the letters. "P.B.C.!"

The Space Lizard snarled and pulled back the lever on his ray gun. The barrel's bubble bulges began throbbing with colored light.

"Hurry!" shouted Farkas. "He's charging his blaster. We only have like thirty seconds."

Billy was confused. "What does 'P.B.C.' mean?"

The acid blaster was aimed at Farkas, who was shielding Pollyanna.

"It's short for 'peanut butter crackers'! " Farkas shouted over his shoulder.

"You fight this monster with snack food?" said Walter.

"Yes, Waldo! The Space Lizard thinks they're square orange eggs. He gobbles them down. The crackers are so dry they soak up his saliva. It's like he has this huge acid-packed sponge in his mouth and then—*BOOM!*—he explodes."

Billy typed in the words, then read them out loud: " 'Peanut butter crackers'!"

Nothing happened.

The lizard's warbling weapon was almost fully charged.

Billy dropped to his knees, rummaged through his backpack, and found his emergency packs of "P.B.C.s." As fast as he could, he started reading the ingredients printed on the back.

“ ‘Enriched flour, riboflavin, folic acid, peanut butter, soybean oil with TBHQ for freshness—’ ”

Eight floating orange cracker sandwiches the size of pizza boxes appeared in the air around the Space Lizard’s head. They rotated slowly and looked like hovering throw pillows from a couch—but with airholes instead of buttons.

“Oh my,” said Pollyanna, stepping right up to the lizard. “I imagine you must be very glad to see all these square orange eggs.”

“It’ssss a trick!”

“A trick? Or is it a treat? It all depends on three little letters. Don’t you see? It’s ever so easy to turn a sad word into a glad one!”

The Space Lizard’s eyes bulged out of their sockets.

“Orange eggssssssssss!”

The maniac snagged an orange square out of the air and wolfed it down in three quick chomps.

“Orange eggssssssssss!”

He grabbed another.

And another.

As the monster munched, Billy heard the kind of gurgly sounds a straw makes when someone sucks up the bottom of a milk shake.

“Close your eyes,” Farkas said to Pollyanna. “This Space Lizard is about to blow!”

Down went peanut butter cracker number eight. The Space Lizard’s head inflated like a water balloon connected to a garden hose.

"This next part is awesome," said Farkas.

"Goodness," said Pollyanna. "What happens?"

"His head, his whole body—everything goes *KERPLOOEY*! Duck!"

Farkas yanked Pollyanna to the ground. Billy and Walter covered their heads.

BA-BOOM!

There was a humongous explosion.

Slimy chunks of lizard gristle flew in all directions. So did soggy wads of orange gunk and gobs of regurgitated peanut butter. Pollyanna and Farkas, who were the closest to the blast, were both splattered with dribbling globules of goop.

The Space Lizard had definitely been annihilated.

"Well, I'm very glad *he's* gone," said Pollyanna, daintily wiping cheesy slime off her ruffled blouse. "Thank you for your kind assistance." She popped up on her toes to kiss Farkas on the cheek.

His face turned purple.

"Um, uh," he stammered. "Is there anything else I can do for you, Miss, uh—?"

"Pollyanna."

"Yes," said Billy. "There is."

With the Space Lizard gone, it was time for Billy to concentrate on the most important thing he needed to fix.

He turned to Walter.

"We need a spell to erase Farkas's memory of what just happened."

"On it!"

Walter pulled out his stack of Magical Battical cards.

"Found a Memory Mop spell card," Walter reported.

"Good. Read it."

Walter started mumbling.

Billy went over to Pollyanna and Farkas, who was glaring at him.

"I wasn't asking if *you* needed anything, Weedpole," he said through teeth clenched in a smile. "I was asking *her*."

"Well," said Billy, "I bet what Pollyanna really needs

on a hot summer night like this is a big bowl of chocolate chip ice cream."

"Golly!" she gushed. "It's not even Sunday and you have ice cream?"

"Yeah," said Farkas. "Back at my house. Want some?"

"Why, of course I do. I don't see how anybody can help wanting ice cream!"

"Wait here," said Farkas. "I'll bring some back."

He ran across the field.

A sparkling pinwheel of fireflies flew after him.

"That's my Memory Mop!" reported Walter.

"Excellent," said Billy. "Let's follow Farkas down to the shore. Make sure the spell card works. Good night, Pollyanna!"

He and Walter raced to the gate and down the trail and made it back to the shoreline just in time to hear Farkas say, "What the heck am I doing on this stupid island in the middle of the stupid night?"

Then he fired up his Jet Ski and zoomed home across the lake.

"Woo-hoo!" said Walter. "This thing is going to work."

"Yeah," said Billy.

"However, I do see one slight problem."

"What's that?"

"Farkas took his Jet Ski. How, exactly, are we getting home?"

Billy grinned. "In the boat my parents are about to row over here. Come on. It's time for the main event."

He led the way back to the clearing and H. G. Wells's time machine.

"I'll put the blueberry pie on this shelf underneath the control dials."

"You hungry?" asked Walter.

"No."

"We probably should've packed a snack. Something besides peanut butter crackers. I may never eat those again."

"Walter?"

"Yeah?"

"This pie is for my mom and dad. I'm sending them back fifteen years to when they first fell in love. If there's any pie left when they come back from the past, I'm sure they'll be happy to share it with us."

"I hope so. Hey, you know what?" Walter fumbled through his deck of cards. "We should have the Junior Wizard seek out a love potion—something to make certain your parents *stay* in love. Forever!"

"Good idea," said Billy.

As if on command, the Junior Wizard appeared at the shadowy edge of the forest.

"We need a love potion," declared Walter in his best wizard voice. "Go forth and find it!"

The Junior Wizard shot through the underbrush like a crazy comet.

"It'll probably take him out of the game for a little while," said Walter. "Seeking usually does."

"Okay. You're up next."

"What do I need to do?"

"Call my dad. Tell him I fell off a cliff and sprained my ankle. You need my mom and dad to help you rescue me."

"Cool."

"One of our iPhones should go in the time machine."

"What for?"

"We'll set a 'reminder' alarm for half an hour from now. It'll tell Mom and Dad it's time to come back to the present."

"Here," said Walter. "Use mine."

"Thanks."

Billy typed in the instructions: PUSH THE LEVER FORWARD. He set the alarm. Then he adjusted the dials on the time machine to display the current date and the same summer day fifteen years in the past.

Billy tapped in his dad's cell number and handed his iPhone to Walter.

They both listened as the phone rang. And rang. And rang.

"He's not answering!"

"Give him a minute," Billy whispered. "He's asleep."

After two more *BRRRR*s, Billy heard his father's groggy voice. "Hello?"

"Hi. Mr. Gillfoyle? This is Walter Andrews. I live in the cabin next to Mrs. Gillfoyle's."

"Right. Billy's new friend."

"Yes, sir. That's why I'm calling!" Walter started

sobbing. Billy was impressed. Walter was an excellent actor. "This is so horrible, sir. Horrible!"

"What's wrong?" Billy's father sounded much more awake now.

"Well, sir, Billy and I were hiking and Billy fell off the cliff!"

"Oooh!" Billy moaned, cupping his hands around his mouth to make it sound like he was far away. "Owww!"

"That's him," said Walter. "I think he sprained his ankle."

"Where are you, Walter?" Billy's dad asked urgently.

"On the island in the middle of the lake."

"Walter . . . will meet you . . . in the first meadow," Billy called out in fake agony. "Just past . . . the gate!"

"Tell Billy to hang on," said his father. "I'm on my way."

"Bring . . . Mom!" hollered Billy, giving "Mom" a little echo effect.

"He wants his mother, sir," said Walter.

"Of course. Tell him his mother and I are on our way."

51

"You did great!" Billy said to Walter.

"Thanks. Now what?"

"This is the hardest part of the whole thing. Somehow, we have to convince my mom and dad to climb into the time machine."

"So what are you going to say?"

"I can't say anything. I'm not even here. I fell off a cliff, remember?"

"Oh. Right. So what am *I* going to say?"

Billy stroked his chin and thought hard.

"I don't know. We need some kind of obedience potion or something."

Walter tore the rubber band off his stack of cards.

"The Master Wizard can do it. She can do just about anything!" Walter read from the card. " 'The Master Wizard is a master of all things magical.' "

An elegant wizard dressed in a shimmering cape stepped into the clearing. Her hair was silver, like Fourth of July sparklers, her eyes emerald green.

"Omigosh," said Walter. "It's her!"

"What magic do you require?"

"Can you cast a spell on my parents to make them do exactly what we tell them to do?" said Billy.

"Your parents?"

"Yeah. It's really important."

"Tricky. Parents seldom listen to children."

"Just this once?" said Billy. "And only one command." He held up his right hand. "I promise."

The Master Wizard looked deep into Billy's eyes. "Very well. What magic do you require?"

"Well, when my friend Walter tells my mom and dad to sit on that contraption and pull back on the lever, can you make sure they do it?"

She bowed sharply. "Your wish is my command."

In a flash, the Master Wizard dissolved into a glittering fog and drifted over to the time machine, where she blended in with the moonlight glinting off the brass rails.

"Okay," said Billy, "the second Mom and Dad pull back on the lever, they should fly back into the past."

"Perfect," said Walter. "And when they come back, the Junior Wizard will be here with his everlasting-love potion!"

"Yup."

"Man, you have to work in a lot of details when you make up your own story, huh?"

"Tell me about it."

In the distance, they heard someone approaching. Leaves and twigs crunched underfoot. Flashlight beams swung through the trees.

"Walter?" shouted Billy's dad.

"Where are you?" cried Billy's mom.

"You're on," Billy said to Walter. He dashed off to hide behind the nearest tree.

"This is all my fault," Billy heard his father say.

"I guess we both could've handled this thing a whole lot better," said his mom.

The two of them were following Walter across the open field toward the time machine.

"Where is he?" asked Billy's dad.

Walter pointed toward the shadow of the mountain looming on the horizon.

"Up there. And, uh, I think the fastest way for you guys to reach him would be to climb into that sled thing and pull down on that ivory-handled lever."

Billy peeked around his tree trunk.

His mom and dad were staring at Walter.

"Really?" said his dad.

"Yes, sir," said Walter.

Then Billy heard a wind chime go *TINKLE-TINKLE-GLING-GLING*.

"Okay," said Billy's dad.

"Good idea," said his mom.

And the two of them climbed into the time machine.

"Is that pie down there?" said Billy's mom.

"Looks like blueberry," said his dad as he reached out, grabbed hold of the lever, and yanked it back.

Wind rustled through the trees. The time machine suddenly swung around and around, faster and faster, until it became first a whirling blur and then ghostly streaks of faintly glittering brass and ivory.

WHOOSH!

It vanished.

Billy left his hiding place.

"Amazing!" hollered Walter. "We totally blasted your mom and dad into the past."

Billy glanced at the clock on his iPhone.

"Okay. They're young again. Eating blueberry pie. Falling in love. Maybe kissing and junk."

"I am so glad we're not there to see *that,*" said Walter.

"Yeah. Now let's hope the Junior Wizard makes it back in time with the—"

Before Billy could say "love potion," the Junior Wizard bounded out of the bushes holding a bright purple bottle.

"Is that it?" blurted Walter. "How's it work?"

The Junior Wizard started to say something.

But he froze. His whole body sputtered. His pointy hat went jittery. His limbs stuttered back and forth like he was trapped inside a scratched DVD.

And like the time machine, he vanished.

"Billy?" said Walter. "What just happened?"

"I don't know."

“I shut down the Theta Receptors,” someone said in a deep voice.

A tall man in a white lab coat emerged from the forest. The man’s sleek silver hair was neatly parted and plastered to the side. His eyes were intense behind thick black-rimmed glasses.

“Who are you?” said Billy, retreating a step or two.

“That’s Dr. Libris!” said Walter.

"Hello, Billy. Allow me to introduce myself. I am Dr. Xiang Libris. Welcome to my island. I hope you and your mother have been enjoying your stay at my cabin?"

"It's okay," said Billy. "It could use a TV."

"But you had all those books," said Dr. Libris, staring at Billy as if he were an interesting blob of bacteria on a microscope slide. "And, of course, you had my island, where you could enjoy all sorts of adventures."

"We didn't break anything, sir," said Walter.

"I know everything you boys have done out here." He gestured toward a nearby tree, where one of the miniature security cameras sat, blinking its tiny red light.

"You were spying on us?" said Billy.

"I wouldn't call it spying. Let's just say I was recording data for a very important scientific study."

"So what happened to the Junior Wizard?" asked Walter.

"He's gone. They're all gone." Dr. Libris pointed to the wire mesh dome suspended over their heads. "I deactivated the Theta Wave Receptor Grid."

"The what?" said Billy.

"It's all rather complicated. Even your mother would have difficulty comprehending the full scope of the mathematical theorems governing the operation of my invention."

"Try me."

"Very well." Dr. Libris smiled at Billy as if he were an infant. "The brain's theta waves operate in the borderland between the conscious and subconscious worlds. While in the theta state, your mind is capable of deep creative thought. An abundance of theta waves in a person's brain wave pattern, such as evidenced by the remote EEG I was able to run on Billy's brain—"

"What?"

"The pillow. In your bed. It's lined with sensors."

So that's why it felt so lumpy, thought Billy.

"Billy, your EEG readout indicates that you have what we term a 'magical mind.' "

"He's got a gift, right?" said Walter.

"Oh, yes. Billy's brain generates more theta waves than any subject I have ever measured. I believe this is why you were able to project the figments of your imagination well beyond the limits of the dome. I found the beanstalk reaching up into the clouds to be particularly impressive."

"My sister and I helped on that one," said Walter.

Dr. Libris ignored Walter. "Billy, I knew you had

incredible imaginative powers the instant I saw your answers to my ink blot test."

"And once you had me up here," said Billy, "you captured whatever pictures the books put in my brain with the tin ceilings or the metal mesh in the dome. You made my imagination come to life?"

"Precisely. We needed a magical mind like yours for the Theta Project to reach its full potential. Other children can read things here on the island and the net will catch even their feeble theta waves. Only you, Billy, could send your literary imaginings clear across the lake."

"Why didn't you just do it yourself?" demanded Billy.

"I'm afraid we adults lose our capacity for imaginative flights of fancy as we age. That's why you and your mind are such treasures, Billy. Treasures we will soon exploit to our mutual advantage. If you could so easily conjure up Hercules, why not an aircraft carrier? If you could build a time machine, why not a fleet of luxury automobiles that run on nothing but tap water? This is why I sent you that message in the bottle, Billy."

"You mean 'On this island, you shall find great treasure'?"

"Yes, Billy. *Treasure*. Because you and I are going to be rich. Very, very rich!"

Billy's brain felt scrambled.

"Wait a second. What about my parents?"

"Oh, they're far too old to be of any practical use to us. Your father shows signs of minimal creativity and your mother is familiar with the mathematical theories of parallel universes, but—"

"That's not what I'm talking about," said Billy, trying to block out the loud thumping noise coming from somewhere over the horizon. "Me and my stupid theta waves just put my mom and dad into a make-believe time machine and sent them fifteen years into the past."

"Yes," said Dr. Libris, straining to be heard over the *whump-whump-whump*s. "A brilliantly plotted plan. Kudos on that."

"How do I get them back?"

"Excuse me?"

"How do I bring my mom and dad back from the past?"

Dr. Libris's smile slid into a wolfish grin. "You don't have to stay stuck with those two, Billy. Frankly, you could do much, much better than William and Kimberly Gillfoyle. Why, you could have Mary Poppins for your mother and King Arthur for your father. Better yet—Glinda the good witch and Atticus Finch. Choose the right books and your mother and father will be everything you ever wanted them to be."

"I don't want perfect parents. I want mine. How do I get them back?"

"Not sure," Dr. Libris hollered as the throbbing noise grew closer. "Use your imagination."

"But I need the dome!"

"Pardon?"

"The dome! You need to turn it back on!"

"Impossible. The neural net must remain down for routine maintenance while I fly off to meet with my investors."

Suddenly, the trees started swaying and scattering their leaves as a whirlwind swept across the clearing.

Billy looked up.

A sleek black helicopter with the words "Theta Project" painted on its sides descended into the field.

Dr. Libris crouched down and dashed toward the passenger-side door.

Billy flipped on his flashlight app and shone it through the building's tinted windows.

Inside, he saw banks of dead computer screens and video monitors. Not a single LED flickered on any console.

"There must be a generator somewhere," said Walter. "Maybe back on the mainland."

"That cable your dad's company laid under the lake was probably the power line," said Billy.

"So the generator must be—"

Billy motioned for Walter to be quiet.

Somebody was coming.

The two boys peered into the darkness.

Billy saw a silhouette slinking through the shadows.

It was someone, maybe a boy, carrying a fishing pole over his shoulder.

Billy couldn't believe his eyes.

It was Tom Sawyer!

"You're still here?"

"I reckon I is," said Tom, coming into the clearing behind the building. "You boys find you any treasure?"

"But the Junior Wizard disappeared," Billy mumbled.

"So I heard tell," said Tom. "Me and Robin Hood was just talkin' 'bout that."

"Robin's here, too? How? The dome is off."

Walter nudged Billy. "I dreamt up the Junior Wizard. *You* imagined all the others. Maybe Dr. Libris was right. You have a magical mind!"

Billy didn't know what to think.

"Don't mean to interrupt your ponderin', Billy," said Tom. "But me and Robin was kind of curious—can you crack open a fresh book and read us up some fish?"

"But there aren't any fish—except prehistoric ones—in *The Time Machine,* and that's the only book I brought with me tonight."

"So use your magical mind," said Walter. "Just think about fish."

"We'd appreciate it considerable," said Tom. "Haven't had nary a nibble all night."

"Do it, Billy," urged Walter.

Billy sighed and closed his eyes.

This is ridiculous, he thought.

But he gave it a shot.

He tried his best to think about fish instead of his mom and dad.

After a while, a familiar Dr. Seuss rhyme ran through his brain: "*One fish, two fish, red fish, blue fish . . .*"

"By all the saints in Paradise!" Billy heard Robin Hood cry. "Come, Tom, and marvel upon these most magnificent fish! Why, one is red, the other blue! Ah-ha-ha-ha!"

Tom winked at Billy. "Thank you kindly."

And off he dashed through the trees to help Robin Hood haul in their colorful catch.

“Don’t you see?” Walter insisted as they hiked back to the meadow near the gate. “With you, it isn’t just the island or the books from the bookcase or even the dome!”

“I don’t know if I—”

Walter tossed up his arms. “Would you *please,* before your mom and dad are marooned forever on the space-time continuum, stop doubting yourself? You sound like me before I met you. Did I mention how fast I canoed across the lake tonight?”

Billy smiled at Walter. Then he looked up, straight through the gaping hole in the middle of the wire mesh theta wave dome. If he tried this crazy thing, he’d be working without a net. Literally.

Okay, he thought, *it’s time to crank it up a notch. Because if I want a happy ending, I need to write it myself.*

Billy closed his eyes and concentrated.

Until Walter nudged him again.

"Ooh! I have an idea!"

"What is it?"

"When you bring your parents back, make sure you say that they'll be all lovey-dovey forever—like we were going to do with the love potion. That way, they'll never even *think* about splitting up!"

"No," said Billy. "I'm kind of glad the Junior Wizard disappeared. Maybe Mom and Dad have to do that part on their own, to *choose* to stick together. Maybe they get to write their own story, too. All I can do is try to bring them back with a couple good memories so they have a chance for a happier ending."

Walter nodded. "You're right. It's up to them."

"Okay," Billy said when he'd finished composing his story in his head. "Stand back."

"Will there be another explosion?"

"I hope not. But maybe we should hide over there so they don't see us right away."

Billy and Walter ran to the edge of the forest and ducked behind some thick underbrush.

"Billy?" Walter whispered.

"Yeah?"

"Can you add a sentence or two saying this vine I'm kneeling on isn't poison ivy?"

"No problem." Billy cleared his throat and started narrating. "With a blinding flash of dazzling white light, the time machine zips forward to the present day and lands safely on the island in the middle of Lake Katrine."

Blindingly bright light filled the clearing.

His mom and dad were back, sitting side by side on the driver seat of H. G. Wells's time machine.

"It worked!" said Walter.

Billy kept narrating. "The instant they return to the present, however, the time machine and any poison ivy in the general vicinity disappears."

The sled-like contraption vanished! His parents fell on their butts. An empty pie pan rattled around on the ground.

"Oh, man," moaned Walter. "They ate the whole pie."

"Sorry," said Billy before jumping back into his story. "The jolt of their landing makes William and Kimberly Gillfoyle forget how Walter Andrews tricked them into coming out to the island."

"That's good," said Walter. "Erase any questions we can't answer."

Billy nodded. "They also forget all about their time traveling and the time machine and anything else that was totally weird. All that remains are the happy memories they gathered on their journey back into their shared past. They remember how it felt when they first fell in love."

"Ooh," said Walter. "That last bit was good. Poetical."

"Thanks," said Billy. "The end. The rest is up to them."

Billy's mom and dad looked confused.

"Where are we?" asked Billy's dad.

"I'm not sure," said his mom.

Billy's dad stood up, dusted off the seat of his pants, and held out his hand to help Billy's mom stand.

"Another nice touch," said Walter. "Very romantic."

"I didn't write that bit," said Billy. "Dad did."

"Billy?"

"Yeah?"

"I'm really enjoying this story. It has heart, drama . . ."

"Shhh."

Billy's dad looked around, trying to get his bearings.

"Huh," he said. "I think we're out on the island. In the middle of the lake."

"Impossible," said his mom.

"No, look." He led her to a silvery smooth tree. "Remember? We carved our initials on this old beech."

Billy's mom put her hand on the tree's bark. "So how'd we end up on the island?"

"Maybe we entered one of those parallel universes from your dissertation."

Billy's mom smiled. "Have you actually been paying attention to what I've been doing with my life?"

"Not as much as I should have, but yeah. You have a very beautiful brain, Dr. Gillfoyle."

"Why, thank you."

They were gazing dreamily at each other.

"Billy?" said Walter. "I'm closing my eyes. They sound like they might start kissing and junk."

Billy smiled.

Mission accomplished.

"How dare you look so happy, Sir William!" cried an angry voice.

Billy whipped around.

The Sheriff of Nottingham was stalking through the forest with his dagger drawn. "Didst thou honestly think thou couldst be rid of me so easily?"

Billy was too stunned to speak. He and Walter scrabbled out of the bushes.

"Billy?" said his dad.

"Walter?" said his mom.

The sheriff hobbled out after them.

"Who's he?" asked Billy's dad.

"Methinks he is but a cowardly villain!" cried Robin Hood, swinging into the meadow on a vine.

"You're Robin Hood!" said Billy's mom. "You were my favorite."

Robin Hood did his grand, hat-twirling bow as Maid Marian leapt out of the shadows, her broadsword at the ready.

"You fools!" cried the sheriff. "The two of thee hath, once again, fallen into my trap."

"Nay!" said Marian. "It is thou who hast fallen into *our* trap!"

Robin raised his bow and arrow. "All for one!"

"And one for all!" The three musketeers and D'Artagnan charged into the moonlit field with their fencing foils swirling. Hercules and Tom Sawyer were right behind them.

"Billy?" said his dad again. "Who are all these people?"

"My new friends."

The sheriff was surrounded, but he didn't seem the least bit concerned. In fact, he was grinning.

"There is nothing that any of thee can do to be rid of me."

"Billy?" said Walter. "I think we need that sharkodile again."

"Ha!" scoffed the sheriff. "Thy hideous monster shall not scare me away a second time, Sir William."

"Maybe not," said Billy. "But he might *carry* you away. In my mind, I just imagined him with dragon wings."

Billy did his two-finger taxicab whistle.

From overhead came the leathery sound of flapping dragon wings.

The flying sharkodile swooped down and plucked the Sheriff of Nottingham right off the ground.

"No!" screamed the sheriff. "Curses and foul language! Puteth me down! Puteth me down!"

The sheriff tried to shake free, but it was no use. His pantaloons were firmly clamped in the sharkodile's mammoth jaws. The prehistoric creature screeched merrily and carried the sheriff into the moonlit night.

"Huzzah!" shouted Robin Hood, tossing his hat up into the air. "We hath seen the last of that vile varlet."

"What was that?" exclaimed Billy's dad. "And what if he comes back?"

"I don't think he can, Dad," said Billy. "He isn't real."

"So that guy's not really Robin Hood?" asked Billy's dad.

His mom shrugged. "Maybe, maybe not. Just relax, sweetheart. Lighten up. Go with the flow."

Epilogue

Billy wrote a quick epilogue to make certain his parents forgot all the crazy characters they'd met on the island and all the wild things there—except, of course, the important stuff.

Like blueberry pie.

And how it had felt when they first fell in love and carved their initials in the silvery bark of a beech tree.

All the characters said good-bye to Billy and Walter before the boys left the island.

"If you ever need us again," Hercules told Billy, "you know where to find us."

"We shall be slumbering peacefully betwixt our pages," added Robin Hood.

"Simply open our books and read," said Maid Marian, "and we shall once more be at your side."

Hercules squirmed in his tight leggings and tugged at

the collar of his ill-fitting tunic. "But next time, I hope to be wearing my loincloth and lion cape."

"And," said Tom Sawyer, "I reckon I'll be whitewashing another fence."

Billy and Walter rowed Billy's parents back across the lake.

During the crossing, Billy had a funny thought: Nick Farkas racing down to the Lake Katrine Public Library first thing in the morning to check out every single *Pollyanna* book ever written.

As for Dr. Libris? No way was Billy ever going to work for that creepy loon.

When they reached the dock, Billy's mom and dad climbed out and, holding hands, strolled up to the cabin, laughing and talking the whole way.

"The end," said Walter. "Until tomorrow. I still want to go treasure hunting."

Billy did, too—although he figured he didn't *really* need to find any treasure. Neither did his parents. They all just needed to remember what they already had.

For Billy, that meant never forgetting he had a pretty amazing imagination that could make even the impossible seem real. He could create his own sideways staircases.

"Hey, Billy?"

"Yeah, Walter?"

"Tomorrow, after we go treasure hunting, can we go back to the Red Barn?"

"Why?"

"Well, I'm not one hundred percent certain how your magical mind works and all, but I was wondering: Can you write me up some free waffle fries?"

Billy smiled. "Who knows, Walter? Maybe I can."

Author's Note

Writing this book, I had the chance to go back and reread some of the greatest stories ever told, all of them crafted by masterful magicians, authors who created characters so real and full of life, they will remain with us forever. Here's a list so you can read them, too.

(in order of appearance in the text)

The Island of Dr. Moreau
by H. G. Wells

The Wonderful Wizard of Oz
by L. Frank Baum

The Adventures of Pinocchio
by Carlo Collodi

A Christmas Carol
by Charles Dickens

The Labors of Hercules
by Peisander

The Hobbit (or There and Back Again)
by J. R. R. Tolkien

Moby-Dick (or The Whale)
by Herman Melville

The Adventures of Sherlock Holmes
by Sir Arthur Conan Doyle

The Seven Voyages of Sinbad the Sailor
(originally part of the *Arabian Nights*)

The Merry Adventures of Robin Hood
of Great Renown, in Nottinghamshire
by Howard Pyle

"The Three Billy Goats Gruff"
(Norwegian folktale)

Aesop's Fables
by Aesop

Treasure Island
by Robert Louis Stevenson

The Adventures of Tom Sawyer
by Mark Twain

Aladdin
(originally part of the *Arabian Nights*)

The Hunchback of Notre Dame
by Victor Hugo

20,000 Leagues Under the Sea
by Jules Verne

Pollyanna: The Glad Book
by Eleanor H. Porter

The Three Musketeers
by Alexandre Dumas

The Time Machine
by H. G. Wells

Holes
by Louis Sachar

Alice's Adventures in Wonderland
by Lewis Carroll

Journey to the Center of the Earth
by Jules Verne

The Haunting of Hill House
by Shirley Jackson

"The Fall of the House of Usher"
by Edgar Allan Poe

"Jack and the Beanstalk"
(traditional English folktale)

Mary Poppins
by P. L. Travers

Le Morte d'Arthur
by Sir Thomas Malory

Glinda of Oz
by L. Frank Baum

To Kill a Mockingbird
by Harper Lee

One Fish, Two Fish, Red Fish, Blue Fish
by Dr. Seuss

Thank You . . .

I was very fortunate to have two terrific editors from Random House Children's Books to help me cut out the boring bits and make the magic make sense: Jennifer Arena and Shana Corey.

And before either of them lent me a firm editorial hand, the best first editor in the world gave me all sorts of help: my wife, J. J. Myers.

Speaking of the Myers family, I would also like to thank my agent and cousin-in-law, Eric Myers. Your dad was, and always will be, so very proud of you.

I'd also like to thank everybody at Random House who helped me put this magic trick together: Nicole de las Heras, who has been the brilliant designer for all my Random House books and brought the unbelievably incredible cover illustrator Gilbert Ford to the island; associate publishing director Michelle Nagler; Laura Antonacci and Adrienne

Waintraub, who've helped libraries, even the one in Alexandriaville, Ohio, discover my books; assistant editor and star of the future Paula Sadler; publicist extraordinaire Lydia Finn; and copy chief Alison Kolani (who had to deal with a guy who never aced any of those SAT punctuation tests).

Working on this book, I thought about all those who, through the years, helped me discover the magic of writing.

Mostly, I thought about teachers. Like the one in fourth grade who let me pass around homemade comic books to my classmates.

Or the seventh-grade English teacher who wrote encouragingly in the margins of my composition book, "You will make your living as a writer someday."

And, most especially, my freshman English teacher at Notre Dame Catholic High School in Chattanooga, Tennessee, an extremely cool cat named Schaack Van Deusen, who opened my eyes to Shakespeare, Mark Twain, and a world of wonderful writing. He let me know that writing stories and acting in plays with the drama club were just as cool as playing sports.

If it weren't for these teachers and mentors, this book, and all the others I have written, would never have been possible.

Finally, thanks, once again, to you. As Samuel Johnson so famously said, "A writer only begins a book. A reader finishes it."

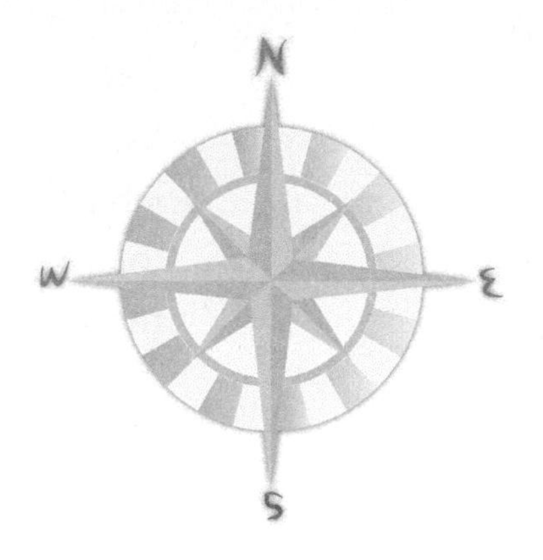

CHRIS GRABENSTEIN

is the coauthor (with James Patterson) of the number one *New York Times* bestseller *I Funny*. He is also an award-winning author of books for children and adults, a playwright, a screenwriter, and a former advertising executive and improvisational comedian. Chris was a writer for Jim Henson's Muppets and is a past president of the New York chapter of the Mystery Writers of America. He also co-wrote the screenplay for the CBS TV movie *The Christmas Gift*, starring John Denver. He lives in New York City with his wife, three cats, and a rescue dog named Fred, who starred in *Chitty Chitty Bang Bang* on Broadway.

You can visit Chris (plus Fred and the cats) at ChrisGrabenstein.com. He also loves hearing from readers, so send your email to author@ChrisGrabenstein.com.